Books by Mark Cheverton

The Gameknight999 Series
Invasion of the Overworld
Battle for the Nether
Confronting the Dragon

The Mystery of Herobrine Series: A Gameknight999 Adventure
Trouble in Zombie-town
The Jungle Temple Oracle
Last Stand on the Ocean Shore

Herobrine Reborn Series: A Gameknight999 Adventure
Saving Crafter
The Destruction of the Overworld
Gameknight999 vs. Herobrine

Herobrine's Revenge Series: A Gameknight999 Adventure
The Phantom Virus
Overworld in Flames
System Overload

The Birth of Herobrine: A Gameknight999 Adventure
The Great Zombie Invasion (Coming Soon!)
Attack of the Shadow-Crafters (Coming Soon!)
Herobrine's War (Coming Soon!)

The Gameknight999 Box Set
The Gameknight999 vs. Herobrine Box Set (Coming Soon!)

The Algae Voices of Azule Series
Algae Voices of Azule
Finding Home
Finding the Lost

AN UNOFFICIAL NOVEL

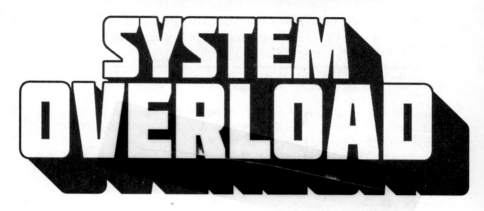

SYSTEM OVERLOAD

HEROBRINE'S REVENGE
BOOK THREE
<<< A GAMEKNIGHT999 ADVENTURE >>>

AN UNOFFICIAL MINECRAFTER'S ADVENTURE

MARK CHEVERTON

SKY PONY PRESS
NEW YORK

Sky Pony Press books may be purchased in bulk at special discounts
for sales promotion, corporate gifts, fund-raising, or educational
purposes. Special editions can also be created to specifications.
For details, contact the Special Sales Department, Sky Pony Press,
307 West 36th Street, 11th Floor, New York, NY 10018 or info@
skyhorsepublishing.com.

Sky Pony® is a registered trademark of Skyhorse Publishing, Inc.®, a
Delaware corporation.

Visit our website at www.skyponypress.com.

10 9 8 7 6 5 4 3 2 1

Library of Congress Cataloging-in-Publication Data is available on file.

Cover design by Owen Corrigan
Cover artwork by Thomas Frick
Technical consultant: *Gameknight999*

Print ISBN: 978-1-5107-0682-8
Ebook ISBN: 978-1-5107-0685-9

Printed in Canada

ACKNOWLEDGMENTS

As always, I want to thank my family for putting up with my obsessive-compulsive need to write. Their understanding and support when I'm stuck on a chapter, or have writer's block, or am just exhausted from typing too much, makes it possible for me to write these books. Thank you from the bottom of my heart.

I'd also like to thank some special people: Christine Jones, Inge Jacobs, and Carol Piotrowski. Without your help, I would never have been able to focus on writing this book, and likely it would never have been completed. Your hard work and dedication is evident in the people you help. They don't always say "thank you," so I'm doing it for them; THANK YOU. We are forever in your debt.

Also, thank you to the great people at Skyhorse Publishing. Their excitement about these Minecraft novels keeps me motivated and working hard. Without their help, I'm sure this novel would never have happened. A special thank you goes out to my editor, Cory Allyn, whose razor-sharp focus and experience are able to stave off all the sloppy metaphors and confusing sentences and make my stories really sparkle and shine.

When you focus on bad things, sometimes that's all you see. If you look for the good, you will find it. The trick is to part the dark curtains of despair, so that the great things around you—like family and friends—can shine through and light your world with joy.

CHAPTER 1
TAKING PRISONERS

The zombie army crouched low behind the sand dunes, waiting to be unleashed upon the unsuspecting village in the distance. The zombies were hungry for battle, and their desire to destroy the NPCs (non-playable characters) that toiled behind the sandstone walls on the other side of the dunes was nearly overwhelming.

"Remember, the goal is to bring back prisoners," the zombie king said. "Do not destroy them unless there is no other option." Xa-Tul walked behind the monsters that huddled in a deep, sandy recession, the iron rings of his chain mail jingling like deadly wind chimes. "Xa-Tul will be disappointed if any zombie gets too excited and destroys when wounding is possible." He drew his huge golden broadsword. The keen edge gleamed in the light of the half-moon. "Xa-Tul will be *very* disappointed."

The monsters knew exactly what the threat implied, and many shook with fear.

"These zombies, under the command of Ta-Vir, will be careful," said a zombie general in gold armor.

"Excellent, General Ta-Vir," the zombie king said. "Be sure all zombies follow the plan. Xa-Tul would hate to see a general punished for any of their failures."

"Yes, sire," the general replied. "Zombies, get ready!"

The golden-clad monster glanced up at the moon overhead. Its half-filled boxy face lit up the desert, making the cactus, dried shrubs, and everything else on the sandy plain, including the zombies, shine with a surreal, almost magical, illumination. But as the boxy clouds flowed across the shining, cratered face, the lunar glow disappeared, plunging the desert into a gloomy darkness.

"Now!" growled Ta-Vir.

Twenty zombies surged out from behind the dunes and ran—as fast as a zombie could run—toward the walled community. They didn't moan or growl or make any noise at all. The zombies just moved as quickly as their shuffling feet would carry them to the sandstone walls and the wooden doors that barred their entrance. Sharp claws tore into the wood, and their clenched fists pounded on the brown timbers.

"Zombies!" a villager shouted from behind the wall in a voice filled with fear.

Xa-Tul smiled, but his toothy grin changed to a frown as archers began firing down upon his warriors from atop the wall.

"Hurry, fools," the zombie king growled.

Zombies flashed red with damage as the pointed shafts fell down upon them. One of the decaying creatures disappeared with a *pop* as its HP (health points) finally fell to zero, leaving behind three glowing balls of XP (experience points) and a piece of zombie flesh. Another monster moved forward to take its place, pounding its clawed fist against the door.

More archers appeared on the wall, firing their lethal rain down upon Xa-Tul's warriors. If they didn't get into the village soon, they would all be destroyed. He had two choices: retreat, or get personally involved. He chose the latter.

Xa-Tul stormed toward his green, decaying zombie horse and leapt up into the saddle. Urging the steed forward, they galloped across the desert, crossing the open territory at a blazing speed. Archers from the wall saw the zombie king approach and opened fire. Their arrows streaked toward him, but bounced harmlessly off his chain mail. Xa-Tul laughed an evil, joyous laugh, then drew his massive golden broadsword as he approached the door. Not waiting for the monsters to get out of the way, he charged forward, trampling a few with his warhorse. When he reached the door, he swung his mighty blade down upon the wooden barrier. It instantly shattered the door into a million splinters.

The zombies moaned with excitement, then charged into the village and stormed up the stairs that led to the top of the wall. Arrows fell upon them like lethal hail, but the growling monsters did not stop. When one creature fell, two more took its place as they attacked the archers with their razor-sharp claws.

"Oh no!" one of the villagers screamed. "More zombies!"

Another fifty decaying monsters surged out of the desert. They passed through the shattered doorway and spread out through the village, seeking NPCs to capture or destroy. Xa-Tul rode through the village on his massive zombie horse. His size and fierce appearance terrified the villagers, causing many to simply drop their weapons and cower in fear. But some chose, foolishly, to stand and fight.

Xa-Tul dismounted and approached an NPC warrior. This villager was clad in iron armor and held a diamond sword—not a trivial weapon. But the zombie king could tell by the way the villager held it that this was no warrior. The NPC was just a pretender who was more afraid of surrender than death. *What a pity for him*, the monster thought.

"Put down the weapon and survive," Xa-Tul growled.

"I'm not afraid of you, zombie," the NPC spat.

"Ha ha ha," the zombie king bellowed, his laughter filling the desert like thunder. "This villager is not afraid of Xa-Tul. He might be right; I actually think he is *terrified*! Ha ha ha . . ."

The iron-clad NPC charged forward, swinging his diamond sword at the zombie's chest. Xa-Tul easily deflected the attack, then kicked the warrior hard in the stomach. The villager doubled over in pain, but stayed on his feet.

Another NPC came running to his friend's aid. This one wore dyed-red leather armor and held an iron sword. He moved in front of his friend while that NPC recovered from the devastating kick. Xa-Tul could see that the newcomer's armor was not as strong, nor was his blade as dangerous, as the first villager's, but the new NPC maneuvered with a deadly grace. He kept his weight on the balls of his stubby feet, always moving rather than just standing his ground. It was just like the way that obnoxious Gameknight999 fought—always in motion.

When the first villager had recovered, the two NPCs split apart, hoping that one of them might get behind the zombie king, where he was more vulnerable. Xa-Tul ignored the iron warrior and focused instead on the leather-clad one.

That NPC lunged forward, his iron sword flashing toward the zombie's ribs. Xa-Tul knocked away the attack, then spun and slashed at the second attacker, whom he could hear charging toward him from behind. His golden broadsword found the villager's shoulder, making him flash red with damage. Not waiting, the king of the zombies spun to the right and lunged at the leather NPC, tearing a deep gash in the villager's tunic. The two villagers now understood their peril, but they kept fighting nonetheless.

An iron sword slashed at Xa-Tul. He stepped aside, easily avoiding the stroke, then smashed his weapon down upon the iron-clad warrior. The NPC flashed over and over again until he finally disappeared, a look of shock and terror on his square face.

"NO!" cried the remaining warrior, who then charged.

The villager slashed at the zombie king with hatred in his eyes. He swung at Xa-Tul's stomach, then poked his iron sword at his shoulder, then spun low and sliced into the zombie's leg. Xa-Tul moaned in pain but brought his own broadsword down upon the NPC. His leather armor disintegrated under the assault. Not waiting for the villager to recover, Xa-Tul attacked again and again, driving the villager back against the wall. Then, with one final swing, he swung his blade into the warrior, tearing away the last of his HP. The NPC disappeared with a *pop* as his inventory littered the sandy ground.

"Are there any more who wish to challenge the king of the zombies?!" Xa-Tul bellowed.

A few warriors were still holding their swords, but at the sound of the monster's voice, they quickly dropped them in surrender. Their defeated eyes lowered to the ground as the zombies moved forward and removed the blades and bows.

With all resistance now eliminated, the surviving villagers were ushered into the courtyard, prodded along with sharp claws. They were herded like cattle around the village well and surrounded by angry monsters.

"The villagers standing before Xa-Tul are now subjects of the zombie empire," the zombie king growled as he paced before them, his gold sword shining in the moonlight. "Xa-Tul now rules all aspects of life. If a villager does not work, then the villager will be eliminated without discussion. Only work will make you free." He turned to one of his generals. "General Ta-Vir, take these volunteers to our zombie-town. Work must be started on the new tunnels before too many zombies arrive."

"Understood, Sire," the general snapped.

With a growl, Ta-Vir motioned for the prisoners to be escorted out of the village and into the desert. The villagers shuffled forward, their defeated faces cast downward. Children sobbed while others moaned in despair, but the cries for mercy fell on deaf ears.

"Faster!" Ta-Vir growled, then swiped at one of the NPCs with sharp claws.

The villager yelled out in pain as he flashed red, taking damage. This instantly motivated the other NPCs to walk faster, for fear that they might become the next example.

They moved through the desert quickly, the only sound being the cries of despair from the villagers. After walking for an hour, the zombies led the prisoners to a hole in the side of a tall, sandy hill. It was a tunnel that extended deep underground.

"Move the NPCs through the tunnels and get them to the zombie-town as quickly as possible," Xa-Tul commanded. "More prisoners are being gathered. These pathetic villagers must be put to work. If they refuse, then they are to be destroyed. Understood?"

The zombies all nodded their decaying heads, then urged the prisoners forward with sharp claws and vicious growls.

"General Ta-Vir, come here."

The golden-clad monster approached and stared up at his king.

"Go back to the village and verify nothing was left behind," Xa-Tul commanded. "Make sure there is no trace that zombies were ever there. Pick up any zombie flesh or XP. Destroy all the animals and take all the XP and food. The village must be completely empty. Take all evidence that NPCs were ever there as well. It is important that the village appears as if it were deserted long ago. We cannot let anyone know what we are doing, especially that awful User-that-is-not-a-user."

"Yes, Sire," the general replied, then turned and began shuffling back to the village.

Xa-Tul watched his commander disappear into the darkness, then looked up at the waning moon.

"I have a little surprise for you, Gameknight999!" the zombie king yelled into the darkness. "A belated gift from your nemesis, Herobrine . . . his final revenge. I only hope the User-that-is-not-a-user is still around to see it. It would bring joy to Xa-Tul to know that Gameknight999 was destroyed at the same time as all of Minecraft."

He laughed a vile, malicious laugh, then turned and followed his zombies into the dark tunnel.

CHAPTER 2

GLITCHES

The ground looked like dirty, shattered brown glass. Hints of red and pink were mixed in with browns. It might have been beautiful in the right setting, but here, in the destroyed forest, it was just sad.

Gameknight999 pulled out his newly-enchanted diamond shovel. Crafter had put the *Efficiency V* enchantment on it, allowing him to dig faster. Placing the tip of the tool on the jagged ground, he was surprised to find that the shovel had dug through five blocks with a single push.

"Wow!" the User-that-is-not-a-user said.

"What?" asked Hunter, to his left.

Her long, flowing crimson curls spilled down her head and across her shoulders. They bounced like a million tiny red springs as she worked. Her deep, chocolate-brown eyes stared at Gameknight999 as if confused for a moment, but when she saw the waves of iridescent light running up the length of the shovel, she understood.

"Ahh, that's the enchanted one, right?" she asked.

Gameknight nodded his square head.

"Lucky you," she growled, then pushed her ordinary shovel into the glassy ground.

The User-that-is-not-a-user flashed her a satisfied grin, then dug up another line of blocks with a single stroke.

They were removing the damaged soil that had been melted and crystalized by the fireballs of the savage blazes. The monsters from the Nether had tried to destroy the Overworld, to eliminate all life here, and then take power. But Gameknight999 and his friends had been able to stop the fiery monsters. Their victory, however, was not without serious casualties: the flaming monsters had done considerable damage to many of the forests, and now it was time to repair what they could and hope Minecraft would recover from its terrible wounds.

As he dug up the shattered soil, Hunter's younger sister, Stitcher, followed behind Gameknight. She placed new blocks of soil in place of the cracked, glassy ones. Behind her came one of the light-crafters, Treebrin. He was a creature that had been created long ago to combat Herobrine's own shadow-crafters. Each light-crafter had an item for which they were responsible. Their task was to improve that item and make it more realistic for the users in Minecraft. In Treebrin's case, he worked on the trees.

Gameknight turned and smiled at the tall Treebrin. He had rough, brown skin that seemed almost like tree bark, and long, stringy brown hair. The light-crafter was easily a head taller than all the NPCs, if not more, with powerful arms and legs that were likely stronger than wood. He was an imposing figure to behold, but his ever-present smile was instantly disarming.

"*Grablach korig*," Treebin mumbled.

"What?" Gameknight replied.

"He said to hurry up," Herder translated. "This forest isn't going to be replanted by itself."

Behind the light-crafter stood Herder with his usual collection of wolves. For some reason, the lanky NPC was the only person that seemed to understand the mysterious light-crafter.

Gameknight flashed him a smile, then turned and continued digging. He cleared out great swaths of ground with the enchanted tool. Stitcher had difficulty keeping up with the User-that-is-not-a-user, whose magical shovel carved into the shattered soil with ease.

"Gameknight, how long do you think you'll be able to stay in Minecraft?" Stitcher asked.

"I'm not sure," he replied. "You see, my dad doesn't really know that I'm here. My parents went out for a while, and Jenny—I mean Monet113—is at a friend's house. So they don't really know I used his invention, the digitizer, to come into Minecraft for real again."

Gameknight paused for a moment and turned to face the young girl. He could see she was staring at the letters that floated above his head, spelling out his username, GAMEKNIGHT999. But then her eyes drifted up into the sky.

"It's still weird seeing your name over your head but no server thread stretching up into the sky," she said.

All users are connected to the Minecraft servers through a server thread. The thread looked like a silvery line of light that stretched from the user's head straight up into the sky. Only the NPCs can see the threads, but Gameknight had none. That was because he was not really logged into the game—he was actually *in* the game. His father's digitizer had transported his whole being into the digital universe so that he could see and hear and feel and smell everything in Minecraft. But this also meant he could also feel pain. It was wonderful and terrifying at the same time. He was a user, but not really in the game, hence: the User-that-is-not-a-user.

"Well, I hope you don't get into any trouble because of this," Stitcher added.

"I'll be OK," Gameknight said. "I just want to help get these forests replanted, then I'll go back home."

"Hey, genius," Hunter said from a few blocks away. "How are you going to turn on the digitizer so you can actually get back into the physical world?"

"Well . . . ahh . . . I'm gonna . . ." A confused expression came over Gameknight's face as he thought about it.

Hunter started to laugh out loud. This caused Stitcher to join in, both of the sisters giggling at their friend. Eventually, Gameknight, too, was laughing.

"I guess I'll wait until someone comes home," the User-that-is-not-a-user said. "Just like I planned."

"Yeah, right," Hunter replied. "Sounds like you really put a lot of thought into this."

Gameknight turned back to his work. He started to dig again, but just as he was about to push the shovel down, he saw the blocks below him flicker for a moment, and then disappear. It looked like they'd been stuck in some kind of glitchy loop for just an instant, then vanished as the enchanted shovel tore through them.

"What the—" Gameknight said softly.

"What was that, Gameknight?" Hunter asked.

"Oh . . . umm, nothing," he replied, scratching his head. All the digging must have made him really tired—he was seeing things that weren't there.

They continued to work on the forest that sat near their village, digging up the melted and shattered dirt and replacing it with fresh soil. Treebrin planted saplings all around them, and Herder followed behind the light-crafter, sprinkling bone meal on the fresh plantings. Many of the saplings burst into full-grown trees; others shimmered with green sparks and grew healthier, but did not bloom into mature pine or birch trees.

As the sun neared the horizon, the workers put away their tools and headed for the safety of the village. Though they saw few monsters these days, it always was a good idea to be safe and get inside before nightfall. Minecraft had a way of punishing the careless.

When they reached the village gates, Gameknight found Digger's twin children, Topper and Filler, waiting to greet him.

"Gameknight . . . Gameknight, come quick!" Topper said.

"Yeah, come see what we found," Filler added.

The boy and girl ran off toward a squat house that sat near the tall cobblestone watchtower at the center of the village. They opened the door to the wooden structure, then waited for Gameknight to catch up.

"Come on . . . we don't have all day!" Filler whined.

Gameknight reached out and tousled Filler's sandy blond hair as he stepped through the door. She stared up at him and gave her idol a huge smile that lit up her face all the way to those bright, blue-green eyes. It made the User-that-is-not-a-user's heart soar with joy.

The room inside the structure was completely empty, with the exception of the wooden chests lining the walls. Each had a sign on them: DIRT, STONE, IRON, LAPIZ, DIAMOND, COAL. . . . Every block imaginable in Minecraft was represented on the signs. Some, like DIRT and STONE, had many double chests, while the DIAMOND chest sat alone off to the side. At the center of the room was a torch-lit hole that plunged down deep into the ground; a wooden fence lined the edge so that no one accidentally fell in.

This was the village's mine.

Gameknight stood, waiting for an explanation from the twins, but instead of talking, the boy and girl just plunged into the torch-lit tunnel. The User-that-is-not-a-user frowned, wondering what this was all about, but followed them regardless. They stopped after descending about twenty blocks, then turned and pulled out their iron pickaxes.

"Watch," Filler said.

She swung her pick, digging the iron tip deep into a stone block. Cracks slowly formed on the face of the cube until it finally gave in. Gameknight heard a soft *pop!* when the cube finally shattered. But the strangest thing happened. The block didn't quite disappear. It seemed to hover there for an instant before finally vanishing.

"Did you see . . . did you see?" Topper asked, his voice squeaking with excitement.

Before Gameknight could answer, the two kids took off again.

"Come on . . . come on," they said in unison as they ran.

The twins sprinted down the cobblestone steps, going deeper in the mine. The User-that-is-not-a-user ran after the duo, having difficulty keeping up with them. Just as he caught up, the two abruptly stopped and repeated their experiment. Gameknight watched as cracks began to spiderweb across the face of the block in front of them, as they had before, until it shattered with a *pop*. But as before, the block seemed to hesitate, a little longer this time, before it finally disappeared.

"What's going on here?" Gameknight asked.

The twins giggled and jumped up and down, then headed even deeper into the mine.

"Wait!" Gameknight shouted, but the siblings did not seem to hear. "Topper, Filler, you know it can be dangerous down here." But it was too late; he found himself speaking only to the darkness. They had already sprinted down the stairs and out of sight.

The User-that-is-not-a-user drew his enchanted diamond sword. The magical power that pulsed within the weapon gave off an iridescent blue light that filled the stairway with an ethereal glow. He knew that zombies could sometimes spawn down here in the tunnels, and he wanted to be careful.

Sprinting down the steps, Gameknight chased after the twins, shouting for them to stop and wait for him. Of course, they didn't; they were just as stubborn as he was. Using every bit of strength, he bolted down the steps, taking many of them two-at-a-time. Slowly, he closed in on the boy and girl;

they were just becoming visible in the distance. As they neared the bedrock level, they stopped and waited for Gameknight999.

"You know you shouldn't be down here by your-selves," the User-that-is-not-a-user lectured. "A zombie could spawn down here or—"

"We aren't afraid of a zombie," Topper inter-rupted proudly. "You taught us how to use a sword, and our dad, Digger, taught us how to use our pickaxes. A single zombie would be no concern, and you know that."

Gameknight frowned, but knew he was right. These two could probably defend themselves against any lone monster down here. But that didn't matter; rules were rules. He was about to reprimand them when Filler started digging again. As before, the iron pickaxe dug into the stone block. Cracks formed and spread out across its face until the block finally shattered. But this time, the block hung there in the air as if suspended by invisi-ble threads for at least a second, and then finally disappeared

"Did you see it?" Topper asked.

"Yeah, it just stayed there after it broke," Filler asked.

"Hmm . . ." Gameknight said.

Suddenly, he could hear voices in the tunnel as many feet pounded their way down the stairs toward them. As they neared, Gameknight could see the village's leader, Crafter, approaching in full armor, Digger and an array of warriors at his back.

"What's happening?" Crafter asked. "Some of the villagers saw you running toward the mine-shaft. Is there something wrong?"

"I don't know," Gameknight said, then turned and glanced down at the twins. "Show them."

The kids beamed with pride, then both pulled out their pickaxes and started to dig into separate blocks of stone. As before, the cubes shattered, but the block of stone hovered there in the air for a second, possibly longer, before disappearing.

"What happened?" Crafter said. "I heard it break, but then it was still there . . . that can't be."

Gameknight shrugged.

"Something is wrong with the server," the User-that-is-not-a-user said. "It looks like it's glitching."

"'Glitching'?" Digger asked. "What is that, and why is it doing it?"

"Glitch means that things aren't working correctly," Gameknight explained. "I saw this once on my own Minecraft server. One day we had lots of people on the server, but I had the software configured incorrectly. The server couldn't handle the load."

"What happened?" Crafter asked.

"First, little things started happening. The server started to lag, then blocks started to behave funny," Gameknight said.

"Like this?" Crafter asked.

He nodded his head.

"Then the games on the mini-game server stopped resetting," Gameknight continued. "I started to notice plots disappearing on the creative server, entire creations disappearing in a blink of an eye. I thought maybe someone had griefed those plots, but then I noticed that the kits on the survival server had gotten all mixed up, as if they were randomly shuffled. Finally, I was playing one of my favorite games, TNT-Defense, and it completely stopped working. We had a big contest going that day. I can remember throwing a TNT block at another player, but instead of exploding, it just landed there on the ground and glowed, like it was about to detonate, but it didn't."

"That doesn't sound so bad," Digger said. "After all, it was just a bunch of games."

"Then a bridge that someone built in the Nether disappeared," Gameknight said, his tone deadly serious. "There were four users on the bridge at the time. They all fell into the lava and were destroyed. If they had been villagers, then . . ." He didn't want to finish the statement. "Redstone mechanisms stopped working. Command blocks did strange things. Plugins stopped working. It reached a point where no one could play on it for a while. I don't really care if a server full of users gets all glitchy, but not one with villagers on it as well. We need to treat this as serious."

"Do the blocks only *glitch* here at this level?" Crafter asked.

"No," Topper said. "They do it higher up, but not as bad."

Crafter shook his head as if he'd just been delivered terrible news.

"What is it?" Gameknight asked.

"You remember when we communicated with the Council of Crafters? We had to use the beacon down here near the bedrock," Crafter said.

Gameknight nodded his square head.

"We had to be down near the bedrock because that's where all the servers overlap and form the pyramid of server planes," Crafter explained. "If the server lag and glitches are worse down there, then whatever is happening is affecting all the servers, everywhere, in Minecraft."

"That doesn't sound good," Topper said, a look of concern in his young blue-green eyes.

Gameknight reached out and messed his sandy blond hair.

"It can't be *that* bad," the User-that-is-not-a-user said with a smile.

He turned and faced Crafter, but he could see worry in his bright blue eyes. What Gameknight didn't mention was what eventually happened to that server, and it was not good.

CHAPTER 3

THE EMPTY VILLAGE

They came out of the mine single-file. Gameknight stayed at the back of the procession with Topper and Filler. The twins were beaming with pride because they had brought this problem to the villagers' attention.

"Was it good we found these glitches?" Topper asked.

"Yeah . . . was it important?" Filler added, her eyes twinkling with excitement.

"Yes, it was very important," Gameknight replied. "You both did a really good job today."

"Is this dangerous?" Filler asked. "Could it mean trouble for our village?"

"No," Gameknight said. "I'm sure it's just a little glitch. These things usually just go away once the servers catch up. It will be no big deal, I'm sure."

He felt bad lying to the twins, but the fact was Gameknight999 had a bad feeling about this. When this happened on his server, the glitches and lag became worse and worse until eventually everything completely crashed. On a silly Minecraft

server like the Gameknight999 Network, it probably didn't matter, but this server was filled with his
friends and with NPCs that were alive. Crashing
might be very bad, if not deadly.

When he stepped out of the mine and into the
courtyard of the village, Gameknight could see word
had already spread through the community. People
in small groups were talking in hushed whispers as
they deliberated over the possible meanings of the
server glitches. He could just imagine all the terrible things they were probably saying.

I wonder if this is linked to me somehow,
Gameknight thought. *All the monster kings were
after me, and then Herobrine chased me all over the
server. Then we had to disable his command blocks,
and finally the blazes tried to destroy the Overworld.
Is this just the next chapter in the destruction that
seems to follow me everywhere I go in Minecraft?*

Glancing around the village, the User-that-is-
not-a-user could see the villagers were getting nervous. All they wanted to do was till their soil, care
for their animals, be with their families and friends,
and live their lives. They didn't want another deadly
adventure with the User-that-is-not-a-user.

"Crafter, we should say something to everyone,"
the Gameknight said. "The villagers seem worried,
and—"

"CRAFTER . . . GAMEKNIGHT . . . COME QUICK!"
meone yelled near the watchtower.

Turning, Gameknight bolted for the tall cobblestone building, sprinting around NPCs and stray animals. When he reached the tower, he found a young
villager staggering out of the building, Stitcher helping to hold him up. He wore a charcoal-gray smock
with a bright sky-blue stripe running down the

center. Gameknight pulled out a block of wool and placed it on the ground, to make the NPC more comfortable, then motioned for Stitcher to have him sit.

"Stitcher, what's wrong?" Gameknight asked. "Who is this?"

"I don't know," she replied. "He came out of the minecart network calling your name."

"Give him some food," Crafter said as he knelt by the youth.

Someone handed him some bread. The boy eagerly grabbed the loaf and began stuffing it in his mouth, taking huge bites to quell his hunger and allow his HP to regenerate.

"Son, what is your name?" Crafter asked.

The boy stared up at Crafter with a pair of sad, brown eyes. His light brown hair was matted with sweat.

"My name is Cobbler, and I need to find the User-that-is-not-a-user," the boy said between mouthfuls of bread. "Am I at the right village?"

Gameknight stepped forward and peered down at the boy. Cobbler gazed up at the letters floating above his head, then glanced up higher, looking for the server thread that was not there. An expression of amazement came across his face.

"It's you," he whispered.

"I think so," Gameknight replied. Some of the villagers chuckled. "Now tell us the problem. Is it zombies? Or maybe spiders?"

"Or ghasts?" Topper added excitedly.

Cobbler just shook his head as he finished off the bread.

"No, it's nothing like that," the boy said. "My village . . . it's disappeared."

"What do you mean 'disappeared'?" Crafter asked.

"I mean everyone is gone without a trace," he replied.

"You mean they left the village?" Digger asked.

"No, everyone, I mean *everyone*, is gone," Cobbler said. "I don't know what to do. Everything bad happens to me, and now this. . . . I'm cursed."

"You aren't cursed, Cobbler," Stitcher encouraged. "We'll find out what happened, right Gameknight?"

She glanced up at her friend, the young girl's warm brown eyes expecting some response.

"Ahh . . . yeah, of course we're going to help," Gameknight replied.

""Great! Come on," Cobbler said.

The young boy sprang to his feet and darted back into the watchtower.

"Wait . . ." Gameknight said, but the boy was already gone.

Pushing through the villagers that clustered nearby, he followed Cobbler, only to see his light brown hair disappear down the vertical shaft that led to the crafting chamber.

"Come on," Gameknight said. "We need to follow him."

Without waiting for a reply, the User-that-is-not-a-user moved to the secret tunnel and descended, sliding down the ladder as fast as possible. He could hear feet and hands on the rungs above him, but in the darkness, Gameknight could not tell who was there.

When he reached the bottom of the ladder, he ran through the passage that led to the crafting chamber. Just ahead, he could barely catch glimpses of Cobbler in the darkness.

"Wait for us!" Gameknight shouted, but Cobbler did not slow.

The User-that-is-not-a-user sprinted onward, dashing through the tunnels that he'd used so many times to get to the large underground chamber. The passage quickly ended in a circular room, the iron doors on the far side standing open. Gameknight could remember that first time he'd met Crafter in this very chamber. It seemed a million years ago, but the memory was still vivid.

Dashing for the iron doors, Gameknight ran down the steps, two at a time, until he reached the floor of the crafting chamber.

"This way," Cobbler said as he pulled a minecart from a chest and set it on the tracks. "Come on, follow me."

The boy disappeared into the tunnel, the metal wheels making a clattering sound as they rolled down the rails.

"I guess we're following," Hunter said when she reached Gameknight's side.

"Looks that way," he replied.

They all grabbed a minecart. Gameknight could just barely see the young boy in the darkness of the tunnel. He had no idea where this Cobbler was taking them or where his village was located, but the minecart network stretched all throughout Minecraft. Users didn't know of its existence; it was one of the great secrets of the Overworld.

Soon, the tunnel led to a new crafting chamber. When Gameknight emerged, he could see tunnels piercing the walls of the huge cavern, with mine-cart rails heading out in all directions. Cobbler stood near one of the tracks, waiting for the User-that-is-not-a-user and his friends.

"Cobbler, can you tell us where we're going?" the User-that-is-not-a-user asked.

But as soon as Gameknight made eye contact with the young boy, he disappeared into the next tunnel.

"He seems very anxious to get to his village," Crafter said.

"Maybe if I shoot him with an arrow, he'll slow down a little," Hunter grumbled.

Stitcher punched her older sister in the arm.

"Ouch . . . I was just kidding," the older sister complained.

"I know. That's why I didn't hit you very hard," she replied.

Digger gave out a booming laugh, then placed his minecart on the tracks and climbed in. He pushed off, causing the tiny metal car to roll forward slowly. When it went over the redstone-powered track, it shot off into the tunnel and disappeared in the darkness, with the rest of the friends not far behind.

After traversing through six different crafting chambers, they finally came to their destination: Cobbler's home. When Gameknight emerged from the dark tunnel, he found the young boy standing in the middle of the crafting chamber, just staring at the stairs that led to the surface. He moved to the boy's side.

"Is this your village?" Gameknight asked.

He nodded his head.

"Then how about we go up and see if everyone is back already?" the User-that-is-not-a-user said.

"I'm afraid," Cobbler whispered. "Why does everything bad happen to me?"

"What are you talking about?" Gameknight replied in a soft voice. "Let's just go up and see how things are in your village. We can solve this mystery, together, just you and me."

"Well, and all of us, too," Hunter said, her voice echoing off the stone walls.

It startled Gameknight and Cobbler, making them jump.

"Oops, sorry," Hunter said meekly.

Stitcher punched her sister in the arm again.

"Ouch," the older sister complained.

"You deserved that," the younger said, "as usual."

Hunter flashed a smile to her sister, then pulled her enchanted bow from her inventory. She notched an arrow to the bowstring and headed up the stairs that led to the surface. Stitcher followed close behind, her weapon loaded and ready as well.

"Come on," Gameknight said as he drew his enchanted diamond sword. "You and me together. It will be alright."

"I doubt that," Cobbler said. "It never is alright when it involves me. It always goes wrong."

The User-that-is-not-a-user looked down at the young boy with sad eyes. He felt sorry for Cobbler. *How can someone so young be so sad and pessimistic,* Gameknight thought? *He has no one expecting him to save everyone, or defeat a bunch of monster kings, or face off against someone as terrifying as Herobrine. What does Cobbler have to complain about?*

"Well, we have to go up and find out," Gameknight replied. "Let's go."

Reaching into his inventory, Cobbler withdrew his iron sword and sighed. He then headed up the steps with the User-that-is-not-a-user right behind. They walked slowly through the tunnels and climbed the tall ladder that led up inside the watchtower. Hunter and Stitcher were ready to climb the ladders to the top of the tower while Digger and Crafter stood near the door.

"Ok, we're all here," Crafter said. "Let's go see if we can solve this mystery."

"I doubt it," Cobbler mumbled.

Crafter opened the wooden door and stepped out into the courtyard, followed by the rest of the party. Gameknight walked out right behind Cobbler and stayed at the young boy's side.

It was night in the desert, and the area was bathed in silvery moonlight. Glancing up toward the dark sky, Gameknight saw the countless stars that sparkled down at him—a beautiful backdrop for the half-filled moon that sat high in the sky.

Bringing his eyes back to his surroundings, the User-that-is-not-a-user noticed how silent everything seemed; it was quiet as a graveyard. No animals or people or anything made any sound, except the constant east-to-west wind that always blew in Minecraft. Gameknight ran to the top of the sandstone wall and gazed out into the desert. He scanned the surroundings, walking the perimeter of the village twice as he searched for threats. From the top of the fortified wall, he could hear the small dried plants that dotted the dunes rustling in the breeze, their brown leaves scraping against each other as they fluttered. Tall, green cactus stood vigil all across the desert like prickly sentinels. Their green, barrel-like bodies stood tall and proud as they watched over the sandy wasteland.

No one else was here, no monsters or NPCs. The village and surrounding desert were completely abandoned.

Going back down to the ground, Gameknight walked to the village gates, but the wooden doors were missing. He'd expected that maybe he'd find them left open, or closed, but not missing . . . why would that be?

Crafter approached and spoke in a low voice.

"I've been all through the village," the young NPC said. "There isn't a trace of anyone ever having lived here."

"You think Cobbler lied about this being his village?" Gameknight asked Crafter, who was now at his side.

"Why would he do that?" his friend said softly. "He traveled quite a ways to get to us and ask for help. It wouldn't make sense for him to do that if he was lying."

"Then what happened here?" the User-that-is-not-a-user asked as he pulled out an apple and ate it. He could feel his hunger dissipate quickly. Crafter did the same.

"Maybe it was endermen?" Digger suggested. He'd walked up behind Gameknight at some point during the conversation. "They could make people vanish without a trace."

"But they would need to be enraged to do something like that," Gameknight said. "All villagers know to look away from endermen and avoid striking them, so as not to anger them and allow the shadowy creatures to attack."

"And besides, all the chests in the village are either empty or missing," Crafter said. "Why would endermen take the NPCs' belongings as well?"

"I don't know," Digger admitted.

"Then who or what did this?" Crafter asked.

"Where are all my fellow villagers?" Cobbler asked as he approached. "Did you learn anything?"

Gameknight looked at the young boy, then shook his head.

"I knew I shouldn't have gone out to gather birch wood," the young boy said. "This is probably all my fault, somehow."

"Don't be silly, Cobbler," Stitcher said. "Why would you be responsible for your villagers disappearing?"

"Whatever's going on," Gameknight said, "someone is trying really hard to keep what happened here a secret. If it were the monsters, why would they want to hide this atrocity?"

"Monsters don't care if we know about their violence," Hunter added. "In fact, they would probably want us to know, to scare us. They have no conscience and feel no guilt. So why keep it a secret?"

Gameknight sighed and gave her a shrug.

"Don't worry, Cobbler. We will find out what happened here and get your villagers back," Crafter reassured. "And why whoever is responsible worked so hard to keep it a secret."

"The reason for that secret is what really scares me," Gameknight said softly.

He turned and stared out into the open desert as cold fingers of dread kneaded his soul.

CHAPTER 4
CAPTIVES

Xa-Tul paced back and forth in the large cave. The green light from the lone HP fountain did little to add much illumination to the chamber. They had to rely on the few pools of lava that sat on the edges of the cave to light the entire cavern.

"These old zombie-towns are pathetic. What were they thinking back then?" Xa-Tul grumbled.

"Some of the elder zombies have said these towns were used during the Great Zombie Invasion," one of the generals named So-Kar said. "Creepers were used to dig out these caves, one of the elders said."

"This information is of no interest to Xa-Tul," the zombie king said. "Zombie-towns are a prison. The HP fountains keep zombies chained to their homes, making it impossible to travel far across the land. With that and the burning rays of the sun, the zombie race has been held captive and punished since that ancient war. When Herobrine's last great plan is completed, the zombies will finally be free."

"It would be a great honor if Xa-Tul could share Herobrine's plan with this zombie," the general suggested timidly.

"It is not important for any of my generals to know the plan. It is only important to follow directions," Xa-Tul growled.

The zombie backed away nervously and lowered his scarred head.

"Where are the zombies and villagers?" Xa-Tul growled.

"Should this zombie go check again?" So-Kar asked.

"No, just go away and stop bothering the king."

"Yes, Sire," the zombie said, and quickly left his side.

Xa-Tul glared at the zombie-town with contempt.

It's so small, so pitifully small, the zombie king thought. *Fortunately, there are many of these caves all throughout the Overworld. When all caves are filled, Xa-Tul's zombies will be brought to the main cave, where Herobrine's Revenge will be realized.*

Xa-Tul was impatient, not only because he was waiting for his new prisoners to arrive, but also about executing Herobrine's final command. He paced across the chamber, veering around the many craters that peppered the ground, growling softly.

"Zombies are coming," moaned a monster near the wide entrance to the cavern.

Xa-Tul strode toward the dark passage and waited impatiently near the opening. He could hear the sound of sharp claws scratching across the stony ground as zombie feet approached. Soft moans drifted out of the passage, then became louder and louder.

Finally, he saw them.

His army of zombies shuffled through the passage with a group of NPC prisoners. Some of the villagers tripped and stumbled on the uneven floor, but those who dropped to the ground quickly felt sharp zombie claws across their arms, yanking them back up into formation.

"Bring the prisoners here, to Xa-Tul!" the zombie king bellowed, his bombastic voice echoing all throughout the chamber.

The zombie army pushed and prodded the villagers until they were standing before their new master.

"The villagers before Xa-Tul are now prisoners of the zombie nation," the zombie king said as he paced back and forth before the NPCs like a predatory cat. "Escape is impossible. Any attempt to flee will have fatal consequences." One of the villagers raised his hand to ask a question. Xa-Tul glared at the pathetic NPC with such venomous hatred that he withdrew his hand and quickly lowered his sad eyes to the ground.

"All NPCs must work in order to continue to live. This is an ancient zombie-town from the old days. NPCs do not know of its existence; only zombies are aware of its location. It has been long-abandoned because it is too small for a full zombie-town. But some visiting zombies will now be using it. All villagers must dig tunnels and caves for these new zombies, as they will be arriving soon. If there isn't enough room to fit all the zombies, then NPCs will be destroyed to make room. Is that clear?"

He glared down at the prisoners and growled, showing his pointed teeth. Most just looked at the ground, defeated. It made Xa-Tul laugh.

"Good . . . now get to work," Xa-Tul grumbled. "General So-Kar, make sure none of the prisoners have any weapons. If a sword or bow is found on anyone, destroy both the weapon and the owner."

In response, a handful of weapons clattered to the ground. It made Xa-Tul laugh again.

"These villagers are like sheep," he said to himself.

Xa-Tul turned to another of his generals, a zombie clad in golden armor and holding a gold sword.

"Ta-Ren, take some of the villagers to the portal room and expand it. There will be many zombies coming through the portals. It is important that they are not delayed because the passages are too narrow. Get them enlarged . . . now."

The general snapped to attention, acknowledging the order. Quickly, Ta-Ren gave out orders, splitting the villagers up in groups and distributing them throughout the chamber. When they began to dig, Xa-Tul motioned for Ta-Ren to approach.

"One more thing, general," the zombie king said.

The general stared up into the face of his master.

"I want you to destroy one of the villagers, just to make an example of them for the others. These prisoners must be properly motivated," the zombie king said. "It does not matter what they do, or even if they are working slowly or not . . . just destroy one. There will be many more villagers coming soon to replace them. It is OK to eliminate one or two just to set the proper tone."

Ta-Ren smiled, his sharp, pointed teeth gleaming in the light of the HP fountain. "It will be a pleasure," the general replied.

Xa-Tul laughed, then turned and walked to the steps that led down to the portal room. Villagers were digging into the walls of the stairway, widening it. When they saw him approach, they swung their pickaxes twice as hard, fear painted across their faces.

"You NPCs are pathetic," he growled as he walked down the stairs.

When he reached the portal room, the zombie king looked upon the three glowing gateways, each portal ringed in obsidian. The purple doorway that led to the Nether did not interest Xa-Tul, but the green portal and the pale yellow portal were of great importance.

He walked up to the yellow one and stared into the sparkling sheet.

"Soon, zombies will be flowing from here into Xa-Tul's zombie-town," the king said. "But the zombie-towns must be ready."

He glanced toward the stairway and saw one of the villagers staring at him, listening.

"Back to work or be destroyed!" Xa-Tul yelled.

The villager quickly turned around and chipped away at the stone wall as if his life depended on it . . . and it did.

The zombie king then moved to the green portal. He stepped into it, then turned around and glared at the NPC, his vision slowly wavering.

"Soon . . . all towns will be filled with zombies!" Xa-Tul shouted as he departed. "And then, Herobrine's Revenge will be realized!"

CHAPTER 5
ANOTHER MYSTERY

For lack of a better idea, everyone piled back into their minecarts and headed back to Crafter's village. During the trek back home, Gameknight felt like he was missing something.

"If Cobbler had been home at the time of the attack, he'd be gone too, and we'd never have known the villagers were taken," Gameknight shouted to Hunter in the cart behind him.

"Yeah, so what?" she answered.

"So how does it help the monsters to keep their activities a secret?" Gameknight asked. "What could they be up to?"

"Maybe I should give you the same answer I gave ten minutes ago: I don't know."

"Oh . . . ahh . . . sorry, I'm just thinking out loud," Gameknight said.

"Maybe you can do your thinking a little softer," she said sarcastically.

"We're missing something," he muttered quietly to himself. "There must be a clue somewhere. This is not just some mistake by Cobbler. Something is going on, and it's important; I can feel it. And if we don't stop it, then more people will be at risk. I have to figure this out . . . everyone is counting on me."

Gameknight imagined what it must have been like for all those villagers. Maybe it was a massive monster attack with spiders and creepers and zombies and endermen. There were still three monster kings roaming about: Xa-Tul, the king of the zombies, Feyd, the king of the endermen, and Oxus, the king of the creepers. Gameknight figured that Oxus just wanted to hide out in his creeper hive under that volcano. He had no reason to attack this village. And beside, it was extremely far from his kingdom.

"It can't be the creepers," Gameknight said in a low voice to himself. "It must be the endermen or the zombies. The spiders no longer have a queen, and the skeletons are leaderless. None of them will work together, and they're scattered all across the server. This was an organized attack."

"Are you still talking?" Hunter asked. "I stopped listening a while ago."

Gameknight ignored her. He had to focus on all the possibilities. But before any idea could galvanize within his head, his minecart shot out into the bright light of the crafting chamber.

When he exited, the User-that-is-not-a-user found the chamber already buzzing with conversation. The NPCs near the minecart tracks immediately began asking what happened and were shocked when they heard the village was found completely empty.

Crafter was the last to come out of the tunnel. When he finally emerged, the young NPC moved to Gameknight's side. By now, more villagers were streaming down into the crafting chamber.

"Everyone seems scared," Crafter said.

"It's the uncertainty," Gameknight said. "An enemy you can't see is much scarier than the one standing right in front of you."

"Maybe the User-that-is-not-a-user should say something," Crafter suggested. "You know, calm their fears."

"That's fine for them, but what about my fears?" Gameknight replied with a smile.

He pushed through the crowd, then pulled a block of dirt out of his inventory. Jumping into the air, he placed the block under his feet so that he then stood above everyone in the cavern. Drawing his diamond sword from his inventory, Gameknight banged it against his chest plate. The diamond armor rang like a gong, filling the crafting chamber with sound. This brought all eyes up to Gameknight. But just as he was about to speak, a minecart shot into the room.

"Someone help!" a voice shouted.

The User-that-is-not-a-user turned and saw an old man struggling to step out of the cart and stand. Two NPCs moved to his side and helped him, each holding an arm as they guided him away from the rails and toward the center of the chamber. Gameknight jumped down and made room for the old man to sit.

"What's wrong?" the User-that-is-not-a-user asked. "Are you OK?"

"I don't know . . . they're gone, they're all gone," the old NPC said.

Gameknight flashed a look of concern toward Crafter.

"First, tell us your name," Crafter said.

"My name is Tanner," the ancient villager said, "and I fear something terrible has happened to my village."

"Let me guess: they're all missing?" Gameknight999 asked.

Tanner's square eyes grew wide with shock.

"How did you know?" the old NPC asked.

"Just a lucky guess," the User-that-is-not-a-user replied as feelings of dread filled his soul.

Tanner stared at him, then noticed the letters glowing over his head. Instantly, he tucked his arms into his sleeves, hiding his hands. But as his eyes slowly drifted upward, the ancient villager saw the lack of a server thread.

"It's you," he said, his voice but a whisper.

Gameknight nodded his square head.

Tanner reached out and took one of Gameknight's hands in his own.

"I came here searching for you," Tanner said. "I didn't know where else to go." He began to sob. "My wife, Milker, and my kids and grand-kids . . . all gone," the old NPC moaned. "How can this be?"

"It will be OK, Tanner," Stitcher reassured. "The User-that-is-not-a-user will figure this out. He'll find them, I promise."

Gameknight winced as he felt the sharp needle of responsibility stabbing at him from within.

The old man glanced at the young girl with tears in his eyes and tried to give her a smile, but all he did was cry a little harder. Stitcher looked up at Gameknight, tiny cubes of moisture forming in her eyes.

"We have to do something," she said.

You don't think I know that? Gameknight thought. *But what?*

He nodded his head, then turned away and searched for Crafter. He found the NPC talking with Hunter and Digger. When he saw Gameknight looking in his direction, Crafter joined him.

"Two villages now?" Gameknight said, more of a statement than a question.

"An unlikely coincidence," Crafter added.

By now, the other members of their village had gathered and were all listening to the discussion. Gameknight could feel anger growing amongst the NPCs. With all the conflicts that had blanketed the Minecraft servers over time, the villagers had learned to watch out for each other; any NPC was now welcome in any village. They saw themselves as one giant family, and anything that hurt one village hurt them all.

"We have to go there and see what happened," Digger said. "There must be some clues."

"Digger's right," Hunter added. "We need to investigate."

"Very well," Gameknight said. "Let's gather some supplies and meet in the crafting chamber. Where's Herder?"

"Here!" shouted the lanky boy from the back of the crowd.

"Good," the User-that-is-not-a-user said. "I want you and your wolves with us on this. Maybe they can smell something that we cannot see."

He turned from Herder and scanned the crowd of villagers.

"I'm requesting the help of twenty warriors, just in case we run into trouble. We'll need volunteers. Those who are willing to go, meet us in the crafting chamber after you gather your weapons and armor. Let's do it."

Turning, he glanced at Crafter and gave the young NPC a smile, but there was worry in those ancient blue eyes. . . . Gameknight999 felt the same.

CHAPTER 6

THE PRISONER

ameknight helped Tanner up the steps and through the tunnels. Slowly, they climbed the ladder to the surface of the village. They paused in the watchtower for just a moment, giving the NPC elder a chance to catch his breath. When he was ready, Gameknight led him to the village's well, where he gave the old man some water and food.

As he ate, Tanner glanced about the village, admiring their defenses. "Maybe if we had walls and gates like your village has, then my friends and family would still be safe," he said.

"Maybe," Gameknight replied. "But I've learned that walls are never a guarantee. It's people who keep people safe."

When the old NPC had finished eating, Gameknight took him to the village armory. Iron armor being too heavy for his aged frame, they fitted the old man with a set of leather armor, the tunic and pants colored red.

"Nice dye job," Tanner said to the village's armorer, "but next time you should try this."

He pulled out an ink sack from his inventory and carefully used it to decorate the edges and seams. When Tanner was finished, the plain red tunic now had black piping along the sleeves and sides. It was like something a hero would wear . . . it looked fantastic.

"Never underestimate the value of fancy armor, young man," Tanner said to Gameknight999. "Your opponent might take you for some kind of elite warrior because of it. It might just give you the smallest advantage."

"That's a good point," Gameknight replied. "I think we should get back to the crafting chamber. The volunteers will just about be ready by now."

Tanner nodded as he stood and adjusted the leather armor on his frail body. They headed slowly for the watchtower.

Gameknight went down the ladder first, in case Tanner fell. They slid down the rungs quickly; going down was much easier on the ancient villager than going up. Moving as quickly as possible, Gameknight guided Tanner through the tunnels and to the doors that led to the crafting chamber. He was surprised by the lack of noise they encountered. He had expected to find more villagers heading to the crafting chamber, but the passages seemed empty . . . it was strange.

He stood in the round chamber, waiting for more villagers to arrive, but it remained empty, save for Gameknight999 and Tanner. Now he was getting worried.

With a sigh, the User-that-is-not-a-user moved to the dual iron doors. He banged on the metal with the hilt of his sword, causing a loud *Gong!* to resonate like a church bell as the sound echoed off the polished stone walls.

Slowly, the iron doors creaked open. Crafter stood in front of them, a smile on his face.

"Where is everyone?" Gameknight asked. "We can't go to this village alone."

"Just come in," Crafter said.

"But there might be monsters still at this village. We need to have—"

"Just come in!" Crafter snapped.

Gameknight stepped through the door and was surprised at what he saw. Everyone from the village was assembled in the crafting chamber, all of them in full armor and heavily armed. He was stunned. Every person in the village was willing to go with him to find out what had happened to the missing villagers. He was overwhelmed.

"I don't think you will be alone on this little adventure!" Hunter shouted from the floor of the chamber, a mischievous smile on her face.

Gameknight turned and stared at Tanner. For the first time, an expression of hope twinkled in the ancient villager's eyes.

"Let's do this!" the User-that-is-not-a-user said.

They ran down the stairs, each grabbing a minecart. Tanner led the way, placing his cart on the tracks and disappearing into the darkness, Gameknight999 right on his heels.

As they rolled down the tracks, the User-that-is-not-a-user could hear all the countless wheels clattering on the rails behind him. It was reassuring, knowing that everyone was willing to take this risk with him, but was he putting them in danger by taking them with him?

Why is it that violence seems to follow me everywhere in Minecraft? Gameknight thought. *I must keep them safe, but what if I can't? What if there are too many monsters? What if . . .*

Every terrible thing that *could* happen appeared in his head, chipping away at his courage. He knew he shouldn't focus on the *what-ifs*, and should focus on the *now* instead. But Gameknight was so worried some of his friends might get hurt that he gave in to his imagination, and the thought of all the negative things that could happen made him afraid.

After traversing five different crafting chambers, they finally came to Tanner's village. As with Cobbler's, the crafting chamber was completely empty. There wasn't any sign that anyone had ever been here in the past. It was completely deserted.

"To the surface," Digger said as he ran up the stairs.

The army followed the big NPC like a shining metal snake. They moved, single file, through the tunnels and up the secret ladder until they filled the watchtower.

"Ready?" Digger said as he pulled out his second pickaxe. "GO!"

They burst out of the cobblestone structure and into the village. Archers appeared at the top of the watchtower, while others ran to the top of the fortified wall that separated the village from the savannah.

Gameknight left Tanner and took the ladder to the top of the watchtower. When he reached its peak, he scanned the village. Not a monster in sight . . . nor a villager, other than those that had come with him. But this time, the village was not completely empty. Items were strewn about haphazardly; scattered tools and weapons floated just off the ground.

Sliding down the ladder, the User-that-is-not-a-user walked out of the cobblestone structure and headed for the village well. He found Tanner there, sitting on the ground, weeping. Stitcher was next to him, an arm around his shoulders.

"Where are my friends and family?" Tanner demanded. "What happened? Are they all dead?"

"I don't know," Gameknight said as he peered down at the man with compassion in his eyes.

Crafter suddenly appeared at his side, Cobbler close behind. The young shoemaker had taken to following the older NPC everywhere he went.

"This time, the village was not scrubbed clean," Crafter pointed out.

Gameknight grunted.

"It looks like there was a battle here, and the villagers were killed," Digger said as he approached from behind. "There are items everywhere . . . weapons and armor all over the place." He stared down at Tanner and softened his voice. "I'm so sorry, Tanner. It appears as if your village was attacked and . . ." He didn't finish the statement.

"They're all gone?" Tanner asked.

Digger nodded.

"No!" Gameknight snapped.

"What?" Digger asked.

"Look around," the User-that-is-not-a-user explained. "There are weapons and armor everywhere."

"Yeah . . . so?"

"But no tools . . . and no food," Stitcher added.

"Exactly," Gameknight said. "Either someone wanted this to look like a massacre to us, or they were supposed to pick all this up and—"

"Everyone, come quick!" a voice interrupted.

Gameknight turned and dashed toward the sound. As he ran, he saw Hunter standing by the wall of the village, her bow and arrow aimed at someone in the shadows. Drawing his diamond sword, the User-that-is-not-a-user approached cautiously.

"Look what I found," Hunter said with a smile.

Gameknight stepped forward to find a zombie tucked away in a shadowy corner, a leather cap on his bald, scarred head.

"This zombie was collecting armor and weapons," Hunter explained. "I cornered him."

An arrow stuck out of the monster's shoulder; another poked out from his side. A third arrow would easily take the rest of the monster's HP.

"What are you doing here? What happened to these villagers?" Gameknight asked as he moved closer to the zombie, his diamond sword ready.

The zombie growled, then grinned, showing his pointed teeth.

"We know the villagers here were not killed," the User-that-is-not-a-user continued. "You're going to tell us where they were taken, if you wish to live."

The zombie peered at the letters over Gameknight's head, then glanced up into the empty sky. He then glared about at the warriors that were slowly approaching and laughed.

"This zombie is not scared," the monster growled. "But rather than tell the pathetic villagers where their friends are, it will be shown instead. Come . . . follow, if the NPCs possess any courage."

The zombie stepped forward. In the blink of an eye, Digger wrapped a rope around the monster, pinning his arms to his sides. The monster struggled in vain, then, realizing the ropes would not give, stopped testing his bonds and stood facing Gameknight999.

Hunter then stepped forward and pulled the two arrows out of the monster's flesh, wiping them on the ground before shoving them back into her inventory.

"You're still one arrow away from meeting your ancestors, zombie," Hunter warned. "Do as you are told, or you might not live through this adventure."

The zombie growled at her, then shifted his hateful gaze back to the User-that-is-not-a-user.

"Follow," the zombie said, then walked toward the open village gates, Digger holding the end of the rope firmly in his hand.

Gameknight looked at Crafter, a confused expression on his face.

"What do you want to do?" Crafter asked.

"We follow," Gameknight replied. "I want to know what's going on here. . . . I have to know. And I refuse to just give up on any villager. We're getting our people back."

Following the zombie, the army moved out across the savannah. Herder had his wolves form a protective ring around the NPCs, with archers and swordsmen placed strategically so they could defend themselves if attacked. But as they marched across the land-scape, following the zombie prisoner, Gameknight's imagination created every deadly scenario that could befall them. He envisioned massive attacks from zombies and spiders—the images played over and over in his head. And the more he thought about the terrible possibilities, the more vivid they appeared in his mind . . . and the more scared he became.

CHAPTER 7

FEYD

The king of the endermen paced across the pale landscape of the End, his dark red body standing out against the sea of pallid End stone. Tall obsidian pillars stretched high into the starless sky, dotting the landscape with their dark forms. Each was capped with a small fire that forever burned. Within the wreath of flames, Feyd could see an ender crystal bobbing about, as if the pink cube were unaware of the existence of gravity.

Glancing across the floating island that was their home, and prison, Feyd could see a group of dark endermen clustered together, apparently in heated discussion. Feyd gathered his teleportation powers, allowing a mist of purple particles to form around him. The strange tickling sensation formed in the back of his head, creating the impression that he was in two places at the same time.

And then, at the speed of thought, he was there.

"What is being discussed?" the king of the endermen said in a high-pitched, screechy voice.

"Rabban here says there is something wrong with the End," one of the endermen said.

Feyd shifted his gaze to the monster and gave him a questioning stare.

"Well?" Feyd asked. "What is *wrong* with the End?"

"I don't think it's the End," Rabban explained. "It's the teleportation particles."

This captured the endermen king's attention. The teleportation particles were vital to their survival. When an enderman teleported across the End, the sparkling teleportation particles rejuvenated their health and increased their HP. It was how they fed, for endermen did not eat plants or flesh like those foolish NPCs in the Overworld. Without the purple teleportation particles, the endermen would eventually starve and die.

"Harkonnen here called me a liar," Rabban continued. "He said I should not bother you, but this is too important for petty arguments. It could be critical."

The accused enderman took a step back from Rabban and his king, his black head cast to the ground. Feyd glared at the retreating monster, then shifted his gaze back to Rabban.

"Show me," the king of the endermen commanded.

"That's what I said," protested Harkonnen.

Feyd glanced at the monster, his eyes beginning to glow white with anger. Harkonnen took another step back and cast his eyes to the ground.

"Coward," Feyd mumbled.

He stepped up to Rabban and looked down on him.

"Show me!" he commanded.

"I can't," the subordinate explained. "It's something you cannot see, but can only feel."

"I just teleported and didn't feel anything," Feyd said.

"That's because you only needed a small amount of HP, and it wasn't noticeable," Rabban explained. "If you needed more HP, you could feel it."

"Very well," the king of the endermen replied. "Hit me."

"What?" Rabban asked as he took a step away from his ruler.

"I said, hit me!"

"But . . . Sire. . . I could not . . . ahh . . . I mean . . ."

Rabban continued to move away from his king, walking blindly backward from Feyd. The king of the endermen calmly followed until the cowering monster had backed himself into an obsidian pillar.

"Now that you can retreat no further," Feyd continued, "you will hit me, quickly, or I will destroy you."

Panic and fear filled Rabban's face, but then an expression of resignation filled his eyes. Feyd could tell the enderman had accepted his fate and knew he had no choice. Balling his dark hand into a fist, he punched the king of the endermen lightly in the chest. The nearby monsters gasped in shock.

Feyd's eyes began to glow white with anger.

"I SAID HIT ME!" the king screeched. "Do it again, as hard as you can."

Rabban swallowed and took in a deep breath.

"Do it . . . NOW!"

The endermen balled his hand into a fist, and this time, hit his king with all his strength. Feyd grunted with pain and stumbled backwards. His body flashed red with damage, and the king of the endermen could feel his HP decrease. Gathering his teleportation powers, he transported himself across the End. When he materialized twenty blocks away, his vision was filled with a sparkling purple mist, but his HP did not increase. Slowly, the teleportation particles faded away, and then only when the last of the lavender embers disappeared did he feel his HP begin to rejuvenate, but it was half of what it should have been.

He teleported back to Rabban, and again, the rejuvenation was delayed for just an instant before the healing effects returned and his HP was again at the maximum level.

All the endermen were completely quiet, unsure what Feyd would do next. Touching the king of the endermen was a crime punishable by death. Feyd, of course, knew this, for he had decreed the law himself. He walked up to Rabban and stared at the monster. Rather than cowering, the creature stood tall, waiting for the inevitable lethal punishment. But instead of striking out at the monster, Feyd took two long strides toward Harkonnen. With lightning speed, the endermen king punched the monster in the chest three times, then shoved him to the ground.

"Cowardice is worse than any crime," Feyd said to the monster on the ground that was struggling to breathe.

He balled his hand into a fist and prepared for one last attack. But this time, Harkonnen glared up at his king, ready for his fate, his fear evaporated.

"That's better," Feyd screeched. "Stand up and stop being a fool." He then turned to face Rabban again. "You are right. Something is wrong with our teleportation powers. My healing was delayed, just as you predicted. How is this possible?"

"I do not know," Rabban answered.

"Well, *General Rabban,* you must find out," Feyd said. "This could be serious. I bet this is some kind of attack by the User-that-is-not-a-user. He has altered Minecraft and is using it against us. He must be found."

The other endermen began to screech angrily at the sound of their enemy's name.

"We have stayed in the End long enough!" Feyd screamed. "It is time we made our way into the Overworld again and reminded the NPCs why they should fear us. It is now every enderman's task: Find Gameknight999, so that we can learn what he is doing to the Overworld. After we learn about his plan, then we will formulate our own response, which will destroy him once and for all. Now GO!"

The dark, shadowy creatures around him began to disappear. They left behind a faint purple mist that sparkled, but it was not as brilliant as before. Now that he knew what to look for, Feyd could see that the mechanisms of Minecraft were under strain.

"We will find you, Gameknight999!" Feyd yelled to the empty sky of the End. "And when you are finally in my embrace, I will teach you new levels of fear and pain."

He chuckled an evil laugh, then disappeared in a cloud of lavender.

CHAPTER 8
TUNNELS

They walked across the savannah throughout the rest of the day and into the night, following the directions of the captured zombie. A few spiders tried to approach the villagers, but the keen eyesight of Herder's wolves and their incredible sense of smell alerted the furry guards to their presence. The gigantic arachnids never made it near enough for the army to even see them.

The wolves had become a vital piece of the army, and Gameknight could see how proud the lanky boy was in his furry companions.

"I don't know if I've said it before," Gameknight said, "but nice job with the wolves."

"Thanks," Herder replied, blushing.

Some of the warriors laughed, then patted the boy on the back.

"Gameknight, you said you have your own Minecraft server in the physical world, right?" Herder asked quietly.

"Ahh . . . yeah, sure, but what does that have to—"

"Are there a lot of wolves on it?" the boy inquired. "I would love to see it some day. Can you tell me about it? Are there games? What is your favorite one?"

Gameknight smiled.

"Yeah, there are games," he replied. "I think my favorite one is TNT-Run."

"What's that like?" Herder queried.

"Well, you run over a sheet of TNT. The blocks explode right after you've run over them. The goal is to make it so the other players can't run anymore and they fall through the floor. It's kinda like follow-the-leader with TNT, but the exploding blocks are doing the following, and if you don't run fast enough . . . it's over."

"That sounds fun," the young boy said with a smile.

They walked along in silence as they moved through the savannah. Twisted and bent acacia trees dotted the landscape like living sculptures, each contorted in their own unique shape.

By the time the moon was high overhead, the zombie had reached the base of a large hill, where a dark cave loomed before them.

"Zombie-town is through there," the monster said with a moan.

Gameknight moved to the mouth of the cave and peered in. It was pitch-black in the passage. His imagination conjured up creatures hiding in the shadows, waiting to ensnare the unwary. It all gave him a bad feeling. Stepping away from the opening, he approached Crafter.

"I don't like this," the User-that-is-not-a-user said.

"I know. Neither do I," the young NPC said.

"Why is this monster helping us, anyway?" Hunter asked in a low voice. "The zombies hate us more than just about anything in the world. It makes no sense that this one would show us where the prisoners were taken."

"Maybe he thinks there is nothing we can do to help them," Digger suggested.

"Or maybe he just wanted to prolong his life," Cobbler added. He had quietly snuck up behind Crafter and was now standing at his side. "He probably figured that he'd be killed right then and there if he didn't help. So he led us here to keep himself alive."

"We wouldn't have done that," Gameknight said. "We don't murder in cold blood."

"It's just a zombie," Cobbler said in a low voice. "They probably did something to my village as well. Who cares what happens to it?"

"*I* care," Gameknight snapped. "We aren't going to murder that zombie."

"Great, just my luck," Cobbler replied. "The zombie lives, while my friends and family are probably dead . . . look what's happened to me, again." The young NPC lowered his gaze to the ground, then sulked and walked away.

"Cobbler raises a good point," Crafter said. "It's possible that the zombie is just scared, and willing to do anything to stay alive."

"Well, let's see how much he's willing to help," Gameknight said.

He stood and walked straight toward the monster. As he neared, he drew his diamond sword. The zombie took a step back, then bumped into the hulking form of Digger; fear was painted across the monster's scarred face.

"You got us here, now we don't need you anymore," Gameknight said.

"No, the user is wrong," the zombie moaned. "Many tunnels down there. Only a zombie can find the correct path."

"You lie," Gameknight snapped. "There are probably zombies waiting for us in that tunnel right now."

"No, zombies do not guard the tunnel," the monster pleaded. "It is not necessary. This is a secret entrance. Only zombies know about it. There might be spiders and creepers hiding, but this zombie cannot control that. The zombies will not be in the tunnels. They are in zombie-town."

"Well, maybe we'll keep you alive a bit longer," the User-that-is-not-a-user growled. He turned and winked at Crafter, then glared at the monster. "Show us the way, before I lose my patience."

The monster moved quickly to the entrance, then walked into the darkness. Digger had to run forward and grab the end of the rope before the monster moved too far ahead. He yanked on it, pulling the monster back.

"Wait," Digger ordered.

The zombie stopped in his tracks and stood, motionless.

"Herder, wolves to the front and back of the army," Gameknight ordered. "Everyone, keep your eyes open. Place torches only on the right side of the tunnel. Let's move out."

The army moved forward with the zombie at the head of the formation, wolves on either side. The monster led them through the twisting and turning passage. It intersected with different tunnels and passed through many large caverns, each with multiple exits. It was like a labyrinth; Gameknight half-expected to find the Minotaur waiting for them, but thankfully, that was Greek mythology and not Minecraft. He now understood why they didn't bother to guard it. Without the zombie, there was no hope that the villagers would have ever found the correct way down.

As they moved through the maze, the smell of smoke began to grow in the air. Gameknight knew this meant they were getting close to the level of lava. Soot and ash started to cover the ground more and more as they made their way deeper underground. With every step now, tiny little black clouds puffed up into the air as their feet disturbed the dark coating on the floor. The ash bit into their throats with every breath, making the air taste sour and acrid. But Gameknight knew they had to push on.

Finally, they reached a tall chamber with a stream of lava pouring out of a hole in the wall. The molten stone oozed downward until it flowed across the ground, merging with a trickling stream. A sheet of black obsidian formed where the two liquids clashed. Across the dark plane, an unusually flat wall stood tall in the orange light of the boiling rock. But looking closer, Gameknight could see that it was not completely flat; there was a single block of stone that stuck out.

"There . . . the block," the zombie moaned. "Push it."

Gameknight remembered this kind of entrance from when he had rescued his sister, Monet113, from the zombie-town near Crafter's village.

Moving to the block, he pushed on the stone. It moved just the slightest bit. Instantly, the walls begin to shake, and the sound of stone grinding against stone filled the air. Slowly, a section of the wall began to slide sideways, revealing a dark passage that led into another chamber.

Gameknight ran forward before the rocky door was done moving, dashing through the dark tunnel as soon as he could fit through. The orange light from the nearby lava stream provided just enough light to see the ground, making it possible for him to avoid any holes that might be just out of sight in the darkness.

When he reached the end of the passage, he stopped and hid in the shadows. Before him lay a gigantic cave filled with homes of different sizes and shapes. Each seemed as if they were built from different materials. Likely, every kind of natural block was represented here in zombie-town.

"I always wondered what endermen did with the blocks they stole," Crafter said at his side. "Likely, they brought them to these zombie-towns."

Gameknight grunted and nodded his head.

The small houses lined the edges of the cavern and crept inward toward the middle of the cave, stopping short of the center. A clear space was formed in the center: their gathering area. In the middle was a platform made of obsidian. Gameknight couldn't tell how large it was, but he could still remember the zombie king, Xa-Tul, standing on one similar to that, right before he rescued his sister.

Sparkling green HP fountains dotted the perimeter of the gathering area, the green embers splashing on the ground, then disappearing. Gameknight recalled seeing these fountains in the other zombie-towns, but for some reason, these ones didn't appear as if they were working correctly. Instead of a constant stream of emerald sparks cascading up into the air, these fountains sputtered and faltered, like a squirt-gun without enough water. Gameknight was just about to mention it to Crafter when a sorrowful moan echoed through the chamber.

"Keep that zombie quiet," Gameknight whispered to those behind him.

"That wasn't our zombie," Digger said. "It came from somewhere in the zombie-town."

Gameknight gazed across the chamber. He could see movement near the far wall. Zombies were coming out of a tunnel that descended into darkness. A handful of the monsters shuffled up the stairs, then moved to the nearest HP fountain. The decaying creatures stood within the emerald shower and absorbed the green sparks, rejuvenating their HP. After a few minutes, they moved back into the dark passage and disappeared from sight.

"Come on," the User-that-is-not-a-user said. "Leave some guards here with the zombie. Make sure it stays quiet, or else."

Digger nodded, then assigned some of the villagers to watch over their prisoner. When he returned, the army moved down the stairs that led to the floor of the chamber. They ran between the buildings that seemed randomly placed across the cavern floor. Everyone was on edge, expecting monsters to jump out of every doorway or come charging around every corner. But surprisingly, they encountered no attackers as they wove their way through the disorganized community.

Finally, the NPC army reached the far side of the cavern. Gameknight moved along the rough-hewn wall and approached the dark passage where the zombies had emerged. He could hear their growls and moans down in the shadows, but he couldn't tell how many were there. Some of the warriors moved to the front of the tunnel, ready to charge down, but the User-that-is-not-a-user waved them back. He wasn't sure of the size of their force and didn't want to take any chances. He knew they had a sizable force with them, but he still wanted to be careful.

"I'll go and see how many zombies are down there," Gameknight whispered to a group of NPCs. "Everyone be ready and stay quiet."

Crafter nodded his head, then turned and whispered to Digger, who relayed the message to the next, and so on down the line. Gameknight patted his friend on the shoulder, then headed towards the stone stairway, his diamond sword in his hand. But after descending three steps, he felt a cold, wet nose nuzzle against his left hand. Looking down, he saw a wolf at his side. Glancing over his shoulder, he found Herder grinning a massive smile. Gameknight chuckled, then headed down the stairway, the wolf with him for protection.

He walked down a dozen steps into darkness. The moans of the zombies grew louder as he descended; their sorrowful wails filled the air with a sadness that bespoke the agony of their lives. These were creatures that only knew despair and misery, and wanted all creatures to share in their anguish.

As he grew closer, Gameknight began to identify individual monsters in the growling echoes. Gripping his sword firmly, he followed the passage as it turned to the right, then continued as it plunged downward.

The end of the stairway was now visible. Apparently, the steps led into a large, well-lit room, though the color of the light was strange. It was a mustard yellowish-brown illumination, as if it were a mixture of multiple flickering light sources.

Gameknight moved to the end of the stairway and peered into the chamber. He saw three large obsidian rings, each filled with a different sparkling color: one purple, another green, and the third a sickly yellow. Standing near the portal were fifteen zombies, each covered in gold armor and holding a shining gold sword.

Before he could stop it, the wolf next to him growled, then let out a loud, angry howl. The zombies instantly turned toward the sound and glared into the shadows, their dark eyes filled with hate. And then, all fifteen charged straight toward Gameknight999.

CHAPTER 9

FANGS AND FUR

Gameknight gripped his diamond sword with his right hand, then drew his iron sword with his left.

"I need some help . . . NOW!" the User-that-is-not-a-user yelled.

He could hear his shout echo off the walls as it flittered up the stairs. The sound of boots thundering on the stone steps above him echoed back, but he knew they would never reach him before the zombies did. He could retreat from the monsters, but something inside him refused to do that. Maybe it was pride, or courage, or just stupidity, but he was tired of running from his fears. Gripping his swords tight, he charged forward, the wolf at his side.

Suddenly, a wave of white dashed past him and slammed into the monsters. All of Herder's wolves charged into the battle. They crashed into the green zombies, snapping at rotten legs and tearing deep gashes into golden armor as their sharp teeth sought zombie flesh. The monsters cried out in surprise, then turned away from Gameknight999 to face the wolves.

That was their first mistake.

Gameknight leapt into the monster formation, his swords carving a terrible path of destruction. The golden armor, nicknamed "butter armor" by some Youtuber, shattered quickly under his attack. As soon as the metal coating from one zombie fell away, Gameknight turned to attack the next one, leaving the wolves to finish it off.

Shouts of pain and terror came from the zombies, mixed with the growls of the wolves. The monsters were starting to panic. Sensing their peril, they tried to flee the portal chamber to escape their fate.

That was their second mistake.

As they ran out of the room, they met the NPC army. Soon, they were trapped between the villagers and the wolves, with Gameknight999 slashing away in their midst. The zombies lasted only a few minutes before all were destroyed, their armor and XP the only evidence that they had ever existed.

"Gather the armor," Gameknight said.

"It stinks of zombie," Hunter complained.

"It can be cleaned and will help protect our friends," Gameknight said. He then turned to Digger. "Bring the zombie prisoner."

Digger pointed to a warrior and nodded. The NPC sprinted off, heading toward the cavern entrance. In minutes, the warriors returned with the zombie in tow.

"Where are the villagers that were captured?" Gameknight asked.

The zombie glanced at the zombie flesh that floated on the ground, then glared back at the

User-that-is-not-a-user. His monster eyes widened when he saw the razor-sharp tip of a diamond sword pointed an inch from his chest.

"I can tell when you lie," Gameknight said, hoping his deception was believable. "It is a skill that all users have. We can detect the smallest bit of dishonesty. If you lie to me, then you will join your zombie brothers that were just destroyed. Now I will ask you again: Where are the villagers?"

"Ahh . . . they . . . ahh . . ." the monster stammered.

Hunter stepped forward and notched an arrow to her bow. She pointed it straight at the monster.

"Let me," the redheaded girl said. "I didn't get to shoot any of the ones in the chamber."

"NO," boomed Digger as he stepped forward with his two pickaxes held high overhead, ready for a killing blow. "It's *my* turn to destroy a zombie."

"No . . . wait," the monster cried. "The old zombie-town. They must have taken them to the old zombie-town."

"What old zombie-town?" Gameknight asked.

"Fr . . . fr . . . from the Great War," the zombie stammered. "The king is using the old zombie-towns from the Great Zombie Invasion to keep the plan a secret."

"What's his plan?" Gameknight asked.

He nudged one of the wolves forward so that it was right next to the zombie. The proud animal growled and bared its teeth.

"The king has not shared the plan," the monster said quickly. "All that this zombie knows is that the ancient zombie-towns are being used."

"Show us where these zombie-towns are, if you wish to live," Hunter growled.

"This way . . . this way," the monster said.

Running up the steps, the zombie headed across the open square of the cavern and toward a small opening on the far wall. The narrow tunnel appeared to have been recently carved, with dust and chips of stone still littering the ground. The monster shuffled into the opening with Digger right behind, his strong hand holding firmly onto the rope. Gameknight followed, his enchanted sword and armor lighting the passage with an iridescent blue glow. All he was thinking about were the scared villagers that had been taken from Cobbler's and Tanner's villages.

The passage twisted this way and that as it snaked its way through Minecraft. Gameknight was surprised that it was only one or two blocks wide, unusual for a tunnel made for zombies. They usually seemed to like large spaces with high ceilings and wide passages. Frequently, Digger bumped his head on the uneven ceiling and grumbled a curse meant for the rotting creature at the end of the rope.

The sound of iron scraping against rock was just about the only sound in the tunnel, as armored warriors bumped into protrusions and unexpected cubes of stone and dirt. The User-that-is-not-a-user started placing torches on the wall. About every ten blocks, he would position a torch on the right side of the passage, giving some light to those that followed.

Finally, the zombie stopped short, just as the tunnel opened into a huge crevasse. It was a gigantic, curved structure that looked as if some monstrous being had dragged its axe across the ground, the sharp tip cutting into the landscape and leaving behind the deep chasm. The passage through which the zombie had followed pierced the side of the sheer wall, high above the bottom of the deep ravine.

Gazing to the top, which was open to the sky, Gameknight could see the sun had risen sometime while they were in the zombie-town. But because of the sheer walls of the crevasse, the rays of the sun were unable to penetrate its depths. As a result, the entire floor was shrouded in shadow, allowing zombies to mill about without fear of bursting into flames.

The sound of untold numbers of zombies could be heard moaning below in the shadowy depths. Gameknight could see the monsters moving about on the ground, but the sorrowful wails sounded more numerous than the zombies they could count; there had to be more somewhere.

"Is this it?" Gameknight asked the zombie.

"No," the monster replied. "The entrance to the ancient zombie-town is down on the floor of the crevasse."

"You better not be playing with us," Digger said.

He pulled out a potion of healing and uncorked the bottle. With his free hand, Digger wafted some of the fumes from the potion into the zombie's face. Instantly, fear filled its monstrous eyes.

"This is a healing potion for us," Digger said, "but it's poison to you. Maybe I should pour a little on you to make sure you are properly motivated."

"No . . . no, this zombie speaks the truth," the monster said quickly. "Come, follow, there is a path to the floor."

The zombie gestured down at the sheer wall. At points too far apart for comfort, Gameknight could see the path that the zombie referenced. Cubes of stone stuck out from the wall two and three blocks apart. It looked like a parkour course from someone's nightmare. The path hugged the wall of the crevasse, slowly descending to the valley floor, but any missed step would likely lead to death. This was a dangerous path, but Gameknight knew it was faster than carving their own steps into the side of the sheer wall. He felt like they had to find the villagers, fast, or something terrible might happen.

"Just great," Hunter said sarcastically.

"We can do this," Stitcher said as she glared at her older sister, but it was clear from her voice that she wasn't sure.

Cobbler came to the edge of the sheer face, glanced down at the parkour steps, and then moved back, his young face white as a ghost.

"I can't make it down there," the young boy complained. "I'll probably fall and knock a bunch of you off the steps. This is too dangerous."

"Nonsense," Crafter said. "These steps only have a one-block space between them. That's an easy jump. And besides, you'll follow Digger. There is no way you'll be able to knock him off a step. All you need to do is worry about you and think positively about making it down."

"I'm no jumper, kid," Digger added, "and I know that *I* can do this. It will be a piece of cake for you."

"But what if—" Cobbler complained, but was interrupted.

"We don't have time to debate this," the User-that-is-not-a-user said, a hint of annoyance in his voice.

"Everyone, we need to get moving," he continued out loud to the group. "Be careful, go slow, and you won't fall."

"'Don't fall'," Hunter chuckled. "That's some of the best advice you've given today."

Gameknight was about to respond, but she stepped past him and followed the zombie as it started down. Both easily made the first jump. Digger then moved to the edge and jumped to the first step, with Cobbler following close behind. Glancing over the sheer edge, the User-that-is-not-a-user swallowed nervously, then moved forward and jumped, following Cobbler down the impossible stairway.

CHAPTER 10
NEW INDUCTEES

Xa-Tul paced about the zombie-town in a rage. "The zombies from the other server should have come by now," he growled to himself. "What could be the delay?"

He veered around one of the many craters that pockmarked the ground of this ancient cavern. The zombie king glared at the crater, as if it somehow offended him and needed to be destroyed. The craters were everywhere across this cave, remnants of the builders. This was one of the zombie-towns from before the Great Zombie Invasion. The massive cavern had been made by zombies, who had used creepers to blast open space out of the rocks, which had invariably left holes in the walls and floors. The rough ground was difficult to traverse and added to his frustration.

As he walked toward one of the walls, Xa-Tul could hear the sound of digging. The captured NPCs were widening this cave, just like they were doing to other caves hidden throughout Minecraft. The new zombies would come here, then eventually travel to the largest of the ancient zombie-towns when it was time to execute Herobrine's last great command.

The thought made Xa-Tul smile. When he imagined the fear and shock the NPCs would feel when they realized the trap they'd walked into, it made him laugh.

A splashing sound tore him away from his pleasant daydream. Nearby, a group of monsters waded through the river that ran through the center of the zombie-town. The zombies were trying to get to the HP fountain that sat at the center of the cavern—the only one close by. They bobbed and struggled through the cool waters, then climbed up the bank and shuffled to the HP fountain. When they reached the sparkling emerald spring, the monsters stood motionless with their mouths agape as the soothing embers flowed over them.

But there were so few of the healing springs in this zombie-town. Xa-Tul could feel his rage building again.

"Where are the others?" he grumbled to himself. "There are not enough zombies here."

The zombie king glanced at the tunnel that led down to the portal room; nothing was emerging. Adjusting his chain mail to a more comfortable position, he walked to the passage and stormed down the steps. At the end of the stairway was a large room with three portals dominating the center. He stopped in front of the sickly yellow one. That was the gateway that opened to another world across the pyramid of servers.

A while ago, he'd sent one of his generals through this portal to the other server, with orders to bring all the zombies here to this world, but the idiotic zombie had not returned yet.

"Where is that fool?" Xa-Tul growled to himself. "Perhaps the general, Ta-Zun, was captured and destroyed by villagers."

"What was that?" one of his generals asked.

The zombie king spun around and glared at the monster.

"Xa-Tul was not speaking to Ro-Tir," the zombie king snapped. "Why is the zombie king surrounded by fools? When a response is needed, Xa-Tul will tell the general what to say. For now, if Ro-Til still wishes to live, then stay silent."

The general stepped back into the shadows, out of reach, and lowered his head.

Xa-Tul grunted in annoyance, then continued pacing back and forth. Glancing about the chamber, he saw a zombie near the cave wall. He was a big monster, and looked very strong. This creature wore a gold chest plate and helmet, but no leggings or boots. He had probably not distinguished himself in battle enough yet to warrant a full set of armor. In his right hand, he held a golden sword that sparkled in the light of the portals, its edge keen and razor-sharp.

"Zombie, come forward," Xa-Tul bellowed as he pointed at the monster.

The zombie appeared shocked and afraid. It was never a good idea to be noticed by the zombie king. It either meant that you'd done something wrong or that there was an incredibly dangerous task that needed doing. The monster sighed and slowly approached.

"What is the name of this zombie?" Xa-Tul asked.

"Ki-Lor," the warrior answered.

"Excellent. There is a task for Ki-Lor," the zombie king explained. "Go through the yellow portal to the other server and bring the other zombies here. Tell the zombies that Xa-Tul demands their presence."

"How many should be brought?" the zombie warrior inquired timidly.

Xa-Tul turned his head and glared at the subordinate.

"All of them!" he snapped.

"All of them?" Ki-Lor asked in disbelief.

The king of the zombies nodded his big head, the light from the sparkling gateways reflecting off the crown of thorns that sat slightly to one side of his head, making it appear to glow, as if enchanted.

Ki-Lor moved to the portal and prepared to go through. But just as he was about to step into the insipid, sparkling field, zombies began to flow outward.

"Excellent. They've arrived," Xa-Tul said. "Get out of the way, fool."

Xa-Tul grabbed Ki-Lor and pulled him to the side, throwing him to the edge of the chamber. The monster landed with a thud as he smashed against the wall, his gold chest plate ringing. When Ki-Lor stood, a huge dent was visible in the side of the armor.

The new zombies marched out of the portal, then moved up the steps that led into the old zombie-town. A general, clad in all gold and holding a golden sword, marched up to Xa-Tul.

"Zombies are coming from this other server, as ordered," the general reported.

"Well done, Ta-Zun," the zombie king said. "You are now promoted to Vo-Zun. Go and find these zombies a place to stay."

"Should they be ordered to attack the NPCs?" Vo-Zun asked.

"No!" Xa-Tul snapped. "These new zombies are to stay in the old zombie-town and that is all. Under no circumstance should they go to the surface of the Overworld. Is that understood?"

"But it was assumed that they would be used in an attack. . . ." Vo-Zun began.

Xa-Tul grabbed the general by the edge of his chest plate and pulled him near.

"Are you challenging my decision?" the zombie king bellowed in a loud voice.

"N . . . n . . . n . . . no, Sire," the monster stammered.

"Good! Then do as ordered. Move these zombies into the caves. The NPCs will soon be making them bigger so that more monsters can be housed here."

Xa-Tul stepped aside and watched as at least sixty zombies made their way out of the portal and into the ancient chamber. A grin began to grow across his vile, scarred face. With these yellow portals, he could bring as many zombies here from the other server as he needed, then connect to the next world in the server pyramid and bring even more.

Nothing could stop him now.

CHAPTER 11

THE CREVASSE

The NPCs continued to follow the zombie down the parkour stairway. Gameknight couldn't possibly imagine how this maze of blocks came to be on the sheer wall of the crevasse. Maybe it was just a random occurrence, or perhaps a strange joke from one of the programmers. Or maybe it was put here by Notch himself. He wasn't sure, but right now, he was glad they had a way down, even if it was a dangerous one.

Gameknight gratefully stepped off the last of the parkour steps and planted his feet on the floor. The deadly stairway had deposited them at one end of the curving crevasse, fortunately, far away from the zombies. Moving aside to make room, he stood next to Digger. The growling moans of the zombies were much louder on the floor of the steep ravine, but from what they could hear, most of them were near the center and far end of the fissure.

"What are we going to do with the zombie?" Gameknight asked quietly. "If it yells out, its voice will echo all throughout the crevasse. Other monsters will hear."

"You know what I want to do to it," Hunter said as she returned from scouting the crevasse.

She pulled out her bow and notched an arrow to the string. The enchanted weapon cast a sparkling blue light on the rocky walls. The zombie saw the angry, hateful expression on Hunter's face and took a step back, moaning.

"It's OK, it's OK," a voice said from the impossible steps.

Gameknight turned and found Herder jumping from one step to the next as if falling was impossible to imagine. Behind him came his wolves, the furry white animals leaping from block to block with incredible grace and power.

When Herder reached the ground, he ran to the zombie and stood between the monster and Hunter's arrow.

"I know what to do," Herder said, a little too loud.

"Keep your voice down," Gameknight hissed as the moans of zombies in the distance echoed a little louder, then receded again.

Herder pulled a door from his inventory. He placed it on the ground right next to the zombie, then drew another one from his inventory, putting it adjacent to the first. Two more followed, until they all surrounded the monster. Opening one of them, Herder quickly untied the rope around the creature, then withdrew and closed the door, then placed a block of stone on top of the doors, sealing the creature in from all sides.

"The doors and stone on top will muffle any sounds he makes," Herder explained. "We keep some guards here just in case, then leave the zombie when we're done. He can break through a door eventually and escape. We don't need to hurt him. It's alright."

The lanky boy stared up at Gameknight999, an uncertain expression on his face. He then glanced at Hunter and saw she was lowering her weapon.

"It's a good idea," the User-that-is-not-a-user said.

Hunter nodded, then cast Herder a grin. The zombie within the door-prison moaned quietly, the sound barely audible.

"We'll leave two guards here to make sure the zombie stays quiet," Digger said.

"Agreed," Crafter said. "Builder and Carver, you stay here."

The two NPCs moved forward and stood on either side of the monster, each with an iron sword in their hands. They held them up to the tiny square windows set into the doors, making sure the creature understood their threat.

"Digger, we need a way out of here if things go south," Gameknight said. "Put a bunch of your best diggers on digging a wide stairway up to the surface for our escape. Start from the end of the crevasse here, and head upward."

The stocky NPC nodded his head, then pointed at half-a-dozen big, burly villagers, their arms scarred and scratched like Digger's. They pulled out their pickaxes and started to do what they did best . . . dig.

"Come on," the User-that-is-not-a-user said. "Let's go find our friends."

He moved slowly into the crevasse, staying near the sides and hugging the shadows. As they walked further into the fissure, the sounds of the zombies increased, their growls and moans coming at them from all directions, and growing louder with each step they took. The walls slowly receded as the width of the crevasse increased in size.

"Crafter, do you see the tunnel openings?" Gameknight whispered.

The young NPC nodded his head.

Large holes started to appear in the wall of the crevasse. They extended far into the shadows, the tunnels leading somewhere deep underground.

"Where do you think they go?" Crafter asked.

Gameknight shrugged.

The moaning of the monsters grew in volume as they passed one of the tunnels. The User-that-is-not-a-user glanced at Crafter, then moved to the rocky wall and stood next to the dark opening. The other NPCs did the same, pressing their backs to the walls of the crevasse and hiding in the shadows.

"I think maybe there's a zombie-town down there," Gameknight whispered. It was hard to be heard over the sorrowful moans. "They must have moved from their other town to this one to avoid being seen by us."

"But why would they care if we see them?" Digger asked.

"Maybe we need to go down there and find out," Gameknight suggested.

"That sounds like a fantastic idea," Hunter said sarcastically. "Let's all go down into a dark tunnel filled with the sounds of a hundred zombies. This is one of your best ideas yet."

Stitcher punched her sister in the arm.

"Ouch," she grumbled, then smiled.

Gameknight looked around at the villagers that had followed him on this foolish adventure. Their looks of confidence had slowly been shaved away as they took the parkour stairway to the floor of the crevasse. And now, the loud moans of the zombies were etching away at what little remained.

I can't take them down there with me, Gameknight thought. *Something terrible might happen to them. I don't want to be responsible for that. I must do this alone.*

He turned away from the dark passage and faced the NPCs.

"Not everyone, just me," Gameknight said. "All of you, get defenses set up, in case we need them. We have to be ready for anything. If it goes bad, we can all retreat to the end of the crevasse and use the tunnel the villagers are digging to get to the surface."

"Agreed," the stocky NPC said.

Digger started to give orders. Blocks were placed across the crevasse floor as archer towers began to grow upward. Gameknight marveled at the efficiency of the NPCs, but he knew, sadly, that they'd done this kind of work many times before.

"Gameknight, I have a bad feeling about this," a voice said from behind.

The User-that-is-not-a-user turned and found Cobbler staring up at him.

"What is it, Cobbler?" he asked.

"Everywhere I go, bad things happen," the young boy explained. "I have nothing but bad luck, and I'm afraid it's going to affect you down there in that zombie-town."

"Don't be silly, Cobbler. You don't have bad luck," Gameknight said. "Sometimes bad things happen, but you just need to get over it and keep doing what you need to do."

"That's not very sympathetic," Stitcher said next to him.

"What?" Gameknight asked.

"It's not," she replied with a scowl. "Look, Cobbler, like our insensitive friend here said, bad stuff sometimes happens, but you can always find some good in every situation, if you look hard enough."

"Really?" Cobbler scoffed. "Where is the good thing here? My village, along with my family and all my friends, have all either been taken by zombies or destroyed. I don't see the good part there."

He has a point, the User-that-is-not-a-user thought. *That's pretty terrible. And I wouldn't be surprised to learn that all these zombie attacks are really because of me, somehow.*

"But you're safe," Herder said. "And you told us that your village was missing. If you hadn't been out of the village when the monsters came, then nobody would know what happened, and we wouldn't be hunting for them right now."

"That's right," Crafter added. "I'd say that is pretty good, wouldn't you?"

"Ahh . . . I don't know," Cobbler said as he lowered his gaze to the ground.

"We don't have time for this right now," Gameknight said. "I want to know what is going on in this zombie-town. So I'm going down there to take a peek."

"You aren't going alone," Hunter snapped. "I'm going with you."

"Me, too," her younger sister added.

"No, I need you two here," Gameknight replied. "I want everything ready when I return, in case a bunch of monsters are chasing me. Besides, I can't go stomping around down there with a lot of soldiers with me . . . it will make too much noise, and chances are we'll be detected. No, this is a job that requires stealth and secrecy. I need quick and quiet." He turned and faced Crafter. "I need you to make something while I'm gone."

"What is it?" Crafter replied.

Gameknight explained quietly, sketching on the ground with the tip of his sword.

"I'll have them ready when you return," the young NPC replied.

"OK," the User-that-is-not-a-user said. "All of you, just be ready when I return."

Without waiting for a reply, he spun around and darted into the shadowy passage, a redstone torch in his hand. As he walked, he removed his enchanted diamond armor and replaced it with some of the gold zombie armor they'd collected in the portal room. Gameknight tried to hold his breath as he put it on. The metal stunk of decaying flesh; it was terrible. When he had all the disgusting armor in place, he put away his sword and took out a golden one. Hopefully, this disguise would allow him to get close without being immediately spotted.

Moving as quietly as he could, Gameknight walked down the passage, the redstone torch casting just enough light to see if there were any holes in the ground that he might trip over. His golden boots clicked on the stone floor, and he could only hope it was not too loud. Then he heard something behind him. Spinning around, he raised his sword, ready to attack.

"Hi, Gameknight," a familiar voice said from the darkness.

Holding out the torch, Herder stepped into the dim light, a group of wolves at his side.

"When you said you needed stealthy people, I figured you meant me and my wolves," the lanky boy said with a smile. "So here I am."

Gameknight shook his head and scowled. "OK, stay close and stay quiet," he said. "We aren't looking for a fight. We just want to know what's going on."

He turned and continued down the dark tunnel. It seemed to twist and turn through the stone, gradually descending. The air was dusty and dry, as if fresh air hadn't passed through this corridor for centuries. It dried out Gameknight's throat and made him want to cough, but he resisted the urge; it might get him and Herder killed.

The two friends walked in silence as they moved through the passageway, the soft paws of the wolves making no noise at all.

Gameknight was about to say something when a sorrowful moan filled the air. He stopped and moved against the wall, listening. The sound was distant and not approaching . . . good.

They continued through the passage. Very quickly, it began to slope downward at a sharper pitch as it continued its zigzag path through Minecraft. The sound of the zombies grew in volume, their sad moans now louder than their footsteps. This reduced Gameknight's fear of being heard, but his nerves were still stretched tight.

They skulked through the tunnel, going deeper and deeper as the monster sounds grew louder. Finally, Gameknight and Herder reached the source of the sound . . . the zombie-town. It was a massive cave, but completely different from the one Gameknight had seen when he had rescued his sister. This one had a rough floor that was very uneven, like it had been sculpted out of the ground with TNT. Huge craters dotted the floor of the cave, as if it were a battlefield from some long-forgotten war. A river ran through one side of the town, with zombies bobbing up and down in the current as they tried to cross the watery obstacle. All across the massive chamber, Gameknight could see countless zombies—at least a hundred of them, if not more. They were all clustered at the center of the chamber, where a single HP fountain sprayed out shimmering green embers. The emerald sparks splashed on the ground, coating the nearby zombies with life-restoring HP.

Just then, the pitiful moans increased as a large group of green, decaying monsters emerged from a tunnel on the far side of the town. At the front was none other than Xa-Tul himself.

Gameknight growled, causing the wolves to snarl as well, their white hair standing straight up as their eyes turned red. He watched as the zombie king stormed across the cavern.

And then he saw them!

Villagers were lined up against the wall, each with a pickaxe in their hand. They were digging into the rocky wall, slowly expanding the cavern.

"You see them?" Herder whispered.

Gameknight nodded. "We need to . . ."

Suddenly, a group of three zombies stepped into the passage in front of them. Their dark eyes grew wide when they saw the two NPCs and a dozen wolves. Growls came from the monsters as razor-sharp claws slowly extended from stubby fingers.

"Zombie-town is under attack!" one of the monsters shouted.

The other two charged forward, their angry shouts bouncing off the cavern walls. Gameknight took a step back as he threw aside the gold sword and drew his enchanted diamond blade. Before he could attack the monsters, the wolves dove at them. Strong jaws clamped onto zombie arms and legs, devouring the monsters' HP.

One of the zombies kicked away a wolf and lunged at Gameknight999. But before the claws could reach his diamond armor, Herder was there with his sharp iron sword. The lanky NPC slashed at the monster, hitting it in the arm, then the side, and then the chest. His attacks were so fast, the monster never had a chance to respond. It disappeared with a *pop,* leaving behind three glowing balls of XP.

"No one kicks my wolves!" Herder growled.

Gameknight nodded, acknowledging his friend's ferocity, then turned to face the other two, but the wolves had already finished them off, leaving the passage empty of monsters . . . for the moment. Staring out at the zombie-town, Gameknight could see the entire mob of monsters shuffling toward them. A hundred zombies, or more, were heading straight toward them. There was no way the NPC army could survive this attack.

"Gameknight, what do we do?" Herder asked. "What do we do?"

The User-that-is-not-a-user watched the NPC prisoners for a moment longer, then brought his gaze back to the massive horde of monsters that were approaching. Uncertainty filled him from head to foot.

I have to save those NPCs, Gameknight thought. *But I can't fight all those zombies. I've failed them.*

And as he removed the smelly gold coating and replaced it with his own diamond armor, Gameknight could feel a sense of failure settle into his soul.

CHAPTER 12
RETREAT

"**C**ome on, Gameknight, we need to get out of here," Herder said.

He reached out and grabbed the back of Gameknight's armor, yanking him backward, away from the opening.

"Ahhh . . . what?" he said.

"We need to go," Herder insisted. "The monsters are getting closer."

The wolves began to growl and bark at the approaching mob.

"You're right," the User-that-is-not-a-user said.

He glanced one more time at the NPCs that toiled away with their picks.

"We'll be back!" he shouted to the distant prisoners, but they were too far away; it would be impossible for them to hear him. "I promise!"

The moans of the zombies grew louder.

"Come on, we gotta go," Herder insisted.

"OK," Gameknight agreed reluctantly as he turned and retreated back into the passage.

"Wolves . . . follow," Herder commanded as they took off, following the dark passage, no longer worrying about trying to hide the sound of their footsteps. It was clear that the zombies knew they were there.

When he reached the crevasse, Gameknight found the defenses still under construction. NPCs were climbing up the sheer walls, building stairs that led up to platforms for the archers. Walls were being erected across the entire width of the chasm, with holes for arrows to greet any attacking army and openings that would force groups of zombies into choke points where they'd be more susceptible to the villagers' swords. Digger was using every trick they'd learned from all the battles they'd fought together to come up with a defense that would help them against the approaching storm of claws.

But they have no idea how many monsters are really coming, Gameknight thought grimly.

He sprinted out of the tunnel entrance with Herder right beside him. Behind the duo raced the wolves, their canine eyes glowing bright red. They all sprinted to the structure and shot through the opening. Gameknight and Herder took the stairs to the top of the fortified wall, while the wolves paced about on the ground angrily. The two friends stared at the dark tunnel entrance with trepidation in their hearts.

"Did you find anything?" Hunter asked from one of the tall archer stands.

Gameknight looked up at her. The terrified expression on his square face told her all she needed to know.

"Oh . . . great," she said. "Here we go again."

"I found the captured villagers," the User-that-is-not-a-user finally said. "But I also found a whole bunch of zombies, too, and they're headed this way."

"How many?" Stitcher asked from a hastily-constructed platform on the opposite side.

"You don't want to know," he replied.

"Great!" Hunter replied sarcastically.

Right on cue, growls and moans began to fill the air.

"I think it would be better to run than fight," Crafter said.

"The tunnel to the surface isn't complete yet," Digger replied as he added some blocks to the barricade. "We need more time."

"Then let's give it to them," Crafter replied. "Everyone, get ready!"

The warriors took their places on the rapidly-built fortifications. Swordsmen stood near the openings in the walls, waiting for the monsters to pass through, while archers on the two raised platforms fitted arrows to bowstrings.

"Here they come!" Hunter shouted.

Instantly, Gameknight could hear the twang of her bowstring. Then more strings began to sing as the rest of the archers opened fire. Running across the rampart, the User-that-is-not-a-user moved next to Digger on top of the stone wall. The zombies poured out of the tunnel like a green flood. They were shoulder–to-shoulder, all of them snarling and growling like savage animals as they shuffled forward.

Arrows rained down upon the monsters, but the zombies did not slow or bother to help their wounded brothers. They just charged forward, intent on destroying the intruders. Gameknight put away his sword and pulled out his own enchanted bow. He began firing, but could quickly tell his arrows were not doing enough damage. It was the total sum of all the arrows that were taking their toll on the monsters, but that was about to change. As soon as they reached the stone walls, the archers would no longer have a good angle of attack on the creatures, and the arrows would be much less effective.

The mob needed to be slowed down, and Gameknight999 knew just how to do that, but he was afraid. *Can I be brave enough to do it?* The User-that-is-not-a-user thought. *Can I be as brave as the legendary Smithy of the Two-Swords?* And as he thought about the celebrated NPC, Gameknight felt courage begin to flow through his veins.

Drawing his diamond and iron sword, he jumped off the fortified wall, screaming as loud as possible, then stood out in front of the defensive wall, a lone user facing a hundred zombies. He glared at the monsters the way Smithy would have, with nothing but confidence in his eyes. The monsters saw him step forward, and this unexpectedly aggressive maneuver made them hesitate. The archers took advantage of this and increased their rate of fire.

"It's the User-that-is-not-a-user," one of the gold-clad zombie generals growled, pointing. "Get him . . . ATTACK!"

The monsters took a step back and Gameknght999 advanced a pace. Those at the front of the formation fell under the steel-tipped hail that rained down from the archer towers.

The zombie general drew his sword and smashed it into the monsters in front of him. They flashed red as they took damage.

"Attack . . . NOW!" the commander screamed.

The monsters turned their hateful glare toward Gameknight999 and charged. But to their surprise, the User-that-is-not-a-user just stood his ground.

"Crafter . . . NOW!" Gameknight yelled over his shoulder.

Suddenly, a stream of big, stocky warriors charged out from the defensive wall, each carrying a weapon in their right hand. They formed a line next to the User-that-is-not-a-user, but not so close that they were shoulder-to-shoulder: an important gap remained between each pair of warriors.

"What are you doing?" Hunter shouted. "The zombies will just run right between you!"

Gameknight glanced up at his friend on the archer stand and flashed her a mischievous grin. He then turned to face the oncoming mob.

"Ready?" Gameknight asked the warriors.

They banged their weapons against their metallic chest plates.

The monsters came closer. The stench of their rotting bodies began to fill Gameknight's nose as their sad moans hung in the air.

"NOW!"

As one, the warriors each pulled out a large, rectangular shield. But instead of holding them so they protected their bodies, head to foot, the NPCs turned them sideways, forming a barrier that would block the monsters from running past.

"Close in so there are no gaps," Gameknight instructed. "Hold your ground. We have to give the diggers time to make our escape tunnel." He turned his head and glanced at Hunter. "Fire between us, at the zombies."

She nodded her head as she drew an arrow back and fired it right toward him. The pointed shaft streaked past his head and imbedded itself into an approaching monster. Gameknight turned and struck at the monster with his diamond sword as he held his own shield firmly in his left hand.

"Advance!" Gameknight shouted.

The wall of warriors slowly moved forward. This caused the approaching monsters to slow for a moment, the bravery and audacity of these few warriors giving them pause.

The zombie general began hitting his own troops with his golden sword again, urging them forward. The horde smashed into the wall of shields, pushing the defenders back slowly. Zombie claws raked at the defenses, and tore at those holding them. Arrows flashed over shoulders to strike at the monsters, but there were still just too many of them.

Out of the corner of his eye, Gameknight saw one of the warriors at the end of the line fall. Zombies swarmed over him, then tried to wrap around their flank to attack from behind. But a wave of furry white figures flew out from behind the defense wall and held the line. Herder and his wolves stopped the advancing monsters, keeping the line intact.

Someone cried out in pain as sharp claws found NPC flesh. The person next to Gameknight flashed red as he took damage. The User-that-is-not-a-user slashed at the monsters in front of him, trying to draw them to him, but the zombies didn't fall for his trick and continued their attacks, causing more warriors to yell out in pain.

"Gameknight, we must fall back!" Digger shouted as he smashed a zombie with his pick, then shoved another in the chest with his shield.

"OK," he replied. "Start backing up! Archers: increase your fire!"

As the warriors slowly backed up, the air grew dark with pointed shafts, causing the front rank of zombies to slow.

"Now!" Gameknight shouted. "Everyone behind the walls!"

The warriors spun and bolted for the narrow openings in the rocky fortification, while archers fired through holes in the cobblestone walls, allowing their friends to get behind the defensive structure. Gameknight waited for the others to squeeze through the narrow openings, following them only after everyone else had made it safely inside. Moving along the back of the fortification, Gameknight sealed all of the entrances, blocking the monsters off.

"Move forward!" the zombie general growled. "ATTACK!"

The zombies charged and began to pound on the stone wall. Gameknight heard the stone being chipped away, piece by piece, by sharp claws. Some of the blocks began to show the smallest of cracks. While the decaying creatures smashed their fists against the barrier, others climbed on top of their brothers and sisters in an attempt to get over the top of the barricade, creating a living stairway of zombie flesh.

"They're climbing over the walls!" someone shouted.

"We need to run away," another said.

"No! Stand your ground!" Gameknight shouted. "Our escape is not ready yet. We have nowhere to go." He turned and scanned the sea of faces that were staring at him, their eyes filled with fear. "My friend Impafra used to say, 'If you can't retreat . . . then attack!' Come on!"

He was about to charge forward when one of the diggers from the escape tunnel ran toward them, screaming.

"We did it, we did it!" he yelled. "The tunnel is complete. We can get to the surface."

"Maybe we should choose 'retreat' after all," Hunter said with a laugh.

"Good call. Everyone: RETREAT!" Gameknight shouted.

The NPCs all turned and fled. They bolted to the far end of the crevasse just as the green wave of zombies crested over the fortified wall. As they ran for the exit, Gameknight could hear cobblestone blocks shattering under the assault of zombie claws. Loud roars came from the zombie army as they followed their prey.

At the end of the crevasse, a neat, rectangular hole had been carved into the wall, with steps that disappeared into the darkness. Torches were placed on either side of the opening, pushing aside the shadows of late afternoon.

Suddenly, a loud, booming roar of anger echoed off the sheer stone walls. Gameknight instantly recognized the voice; it was Xa-Tul, the king of the zombies.

"Hurry," Crafter said as he stepped to the side of the tunnel entrance and waited for everyone to pass him.

Gameknight moved to his friend's side and waited as well. He drew his bow and began to fire at the approaching horde; Crafter did the same— but the zombies were closing. Fortunately, their clumsy shuffle caused them to move much slower than NPCs. In addition, Herder had commanded his wolves to harass their pursuers. The wolves were darting in and out of the zombie formation, nipping at a leg here and an arm there, slowing their progress.

When the last of the villagers had reached the top of the steps, Herder whistled for the wolves, then ran up himself amidst a wave of fur.

"Gameknight, go," Crafter said. "I'll seal up the tunnel."

The User-that-is-not-a-user nodded his head and fled up the stairs. He looked back to see Crafter placing blocks of cobblestone on the steps, just as decaying green arms reached toward him. Xa-Tul bellowed another angry wail, his guttural moan stabbing at Gameknight's courage like a rusty knife. This time, the zombies stopped their attack and pulled their decaying arms out of the open gaps in the partially-blocked passage.

Gameknight moved forward and peeked through one of the openings. He could see the monsters turning around and walking away. For some reason, Xa-Tul had recalled his forces, rather than commanding them to continue the attack.

Gameknight glanced at Crafter with surprise on his face. The young leader shrugged, then continued placing blocks of stone until there were three layers of cobblestone and dirt between the monsters and the villagers. When he was convinced that the wall would hold, he turned and ran up the stairs, Gameknight999 beside him.

"Crafter, did we lose anyone?"

The young NPC nodded his blond head. "We lost some," the NPC replied.

Gameknight sighed.

"But it would have been worse if you didn't have us prepare those defenses," Crafter added. "That was good thinking."

"But we shouldn't have lost any!" Gameknight snapped as waves of guilt raked his soul. "This was a disaster."

"What are you talking about?" Crafter asked. "We found our imprisoned friends."

"But they're still captives," he replied. "I didn't do anything to get them free. They probably think I abandoned them."

"That's nonsense," Crafter chided. "They have faith in you, just like all of us do. You'll figure out a way to come back and rescue them, I have no doubt."

Gameknight sighed. He had to figure out some way to get past all those zombies, but it seemed impossible. The only thing he could think about was all the ways they might succumb to the claws of that massive army . . . victory seemed impossible.

"Come on, we'll figure this out later," Crafter said. "Let's get back home and make a plan."

Gameknight nodded as he tried to hide the uncertainty and fear that filled him.

The duo reached the top of the stairs just as the sun began to kiss the horizon, causing the skyline to blush a warm orange, then fade to red.

"Is everyone alright?" Gameknight asked.

He could see many of the NPCs were wounded, and pieces of their armor were cracked or missing. Some of the villagers were weeping for fallen comrades, while others burned with rage.

"I'm sorry that was such a pointless rescue attempt," the User-that-is-not-a-user said solemnly. "All I did was get a bunch of villagers hurt and killed."

"No!" Stitcher snapped. "We did more than that." She stepped forward and glared up at the User-that-is-not-a-user. "We found the ancient zombie town, and we know where our friends are being held. Information is power, right Crafter?"

"She is indeed correct," Crafter replied.

"All we need now is a plan to free those prisoners and stop the zombies at the same time." Stitcher stepped closer to Gameknight and spoke in a low voice. "We need the User-that-is-not-a-user to help us to save our friends. Is the User-that-is-not-a-user I know still in there?" She poked his diamond chest plate with a stubby finger. "Or have you forgotten how to try your best in the face of adversity?"

Gameknight looked down at the young girl, and tried to give her a smile, but all he managed was a sickly grimace.

"When I think of how we might save those villagers and stop the zombies, all I see is disaster," Gameknight said softly.

"You know what I see?" Herder asked in a loud voice. "A problem that has a solution; you just haven't found it yet."

"Gameknight, when I look at you, I see a user that is not afraid to act," Crafter added. "When no one else knows what to do, you are able to come up with something."

"Yeah, but what if that something gets villagers killed?"

"You can't control everything, and you can't ever know the outcome of your choices before you make them," Crafter said. "All you can do is make the best decisions you can, and accept the consequences. But more importantly, we need to look for the positive outcomes, rather than focusing on the negative. You think you just put us all in a terrible battle, and it's your fault, right?"

"It sure seems that way," the User-that-is-not-a-user replied.

"You know what all of *us* think?" Crafter asked.

The other villagers put away their weapons and stared at Gameknight999, their eyes filled with compassion.

"*We* think you found the villagers that were taken prisoner, and you discovered where all the zombies are hiding," Crafter said. "This is a good thing, and yet all you are doing is focusing on the bad. If you want to feel good, then focus on the good. But if you want to feel bad, then keep doing what you're doing now. But I promise you, it won't get you anywhere."

The villagers were completely silent as Gameknight considered his friend's words.

"You get to choose your fate . . . feel good or feel bad. Just choose, and deal with the consequences," Crafter continued, an edge to his voice. "But don't make a foolish choice because you're looking for a reason to feel sorry for yourself. There are people here who care about you and rely on you."

Gameknight knew Crafter was right. A sheepish look spread across his face.

"You know what I feel?" Hunter asked.

All eyes shifted to her.

"Hungry!" she said with a smile.

The villagers laughed.

"What do you say we get back to a village, get some food, and tend to our wounded? Then we'll come back here and take care of these zombies," Hunter suggested.

The villagers cheered in approval.

Gameknight glanced at her and smiled as she gave him a wink.

"OK, which way?" Gameknight asked.

"The closest village is that way," Crafter said, pointing at the setting sun.

"Then let's get moving," Hunter said. "I don't want to resort to eating some zombie flesh . . . I have a feeling that might make me sick."

"Let's go," Digger said. "None of us want to see that."

The army moved out with a ring of wolves around them, heading for the savannah village. As they walked through the darkening landscape, Gameknight thought for a long time about Crafter's advice. . . . *Choose your fate.*

CHAPTER 13

SPIES

Feyd paced impatiently around the End, glaring at the pale yellow landscape that was his prison. His endermen had been sent out into the Overworld to search for his enemy, Gameknight999, but it had been days and the king of the endermen still hadn't heard any news. Frustration grew with every minute he waited, and with each growing moment, he felt an increasingly strong desire to punch something . . . or some*one*.

Suddenly, Feyd realized that he felt momentarily weak. His HP was getting low, and as he was lost in angry thoughts, he had forgotten to replenish it. Gathering his teleportation powers, he zipped across the insipid island to a cluster of endermen. When he materialized, he waited to feel that rush of energy that came from feasting on the teleportation particles that surrounded his body, rejuvenating of his HP, but it was more like a trickle of health than a tidal wave.

A roar sounded from high overhead. The king of the endermen peered upward. The Ender Dragon banked in a large arc as it glided from obsidian pillar to pillar. The ornate cubes that floated in a wreath of flames around the top of the pillars, the Ender crystals, answered the creature's call and shot out a shaft of healing light that hit the flying creature square in the chest. The dragon beat its huge leathery wings as its HP increased.

Feyd felt his energy slowly build as the teleportation particles eventually refreshed his health. He smiled as his HP increased to maximum. But that smile soon turned to a frown.

That took longer than ever before for my HP to rejuvenate, Feyd thought. *Whatever's happening, it's getting worse, and it must have something to do with the User-that-is-not-a-user.*

He must be found, and soon, the enderman king decided. *If the teleportation particles stop completely, then all the endermen will starve.*

As if it could hear Feyd's thoughts, the dragon roared again and stared down at the king of the endermen. Feyd glanced up at the monster and sighed. He wished the dragon still had the glowing eyes of Herobrine, but that had ended when the Maker had been destroyed.

"I wouldn't have thought it would be possible for Gameknight999 to defeat Herobrine in dragon form," the king of the endermen said to himself. "We underestimated you again, User-that-is-not-a-user, but soon your time will come."

The endermen around him looked at their king, unsure if they should respond. But before any could work up the courage to say something, the shadowy monster king teleported again, zipping across the End at the speed of thought.

An enderman appeared before him. It was a smaller creature, not yet full-grown, but already able to teleport with pinpoint accuracy. Something was odd about its appearance . . . something not quite right. And then Feyd realized what was different: it had appeared without any purple teleportation particles surrounding it. As if on cue, the lavender mist then materialized a few seconds later . . . on some sort of a strange delay. Something was definitely going wrong with Minecraft.

There is a mystery here that I don't understand, Feyd thought, *and I don't like mysteries.*

"I have news about the zombies," the creature said, then stepped back away from the dark red king.

Feyd held out his arm and examined it for a moment, then glanced back to the enderman before him. Feyd's skin was a dark, dark red, like the color of dried blood, while the other endermen were black as coal. That was how Herobrine had created him. The Maker, after creating Feyd, had told him the dark red was to remind Gameknight999 of Erebus, the first king of the endermen. Erebus had been created back during the Great Zombie Invasion, a hundred years ago, and had been destroyed by the User-that-is-not-a-user right after his appearance on the servers. Even though Feyd had never met Erebus, he swore that he would avenge the death of his predecessor.

The dark creature before him shifted nervously from one foot to the other.

"Ahhh . . . what did you say?" Feyd asked. "Something about the zombies? You were supposed to be searching for the User-that-is-not-a-user."

"Yes, Sire," the subordinate replied. "Ahh . . . well . . . during my search, I came across the zombies, and they are doing something strange."

"Well . . . are you going to tell me?"

"They are swelling their numbers and creating a vast army. They have abandoned their zombie-towns and have moved to the ancient towns used during the Great Zombie Invasion."

"Why would they do that?" Feyd asked.

The subordinate wisely stayed silent.

"What targets are they attacking?" the enderman king asked.

"That's the strange thing, Sire. They aren't attacking anything."

"What?" Feyd mused. "I don't understand. Explain yourself immediately."

"The zombies are just flowing out of their portal chambers and congregating in the ancient zombie-towns," the young enderman explained. "They have to be coming from somewhere. I assume it is from the other zombie-towns. But when I teleported to the other ancient zombie-towns, I found them all occupied, and they don't look like they're going anywhere anytime soon. All of the zombie-towns are somehow increasing their numbers, and with their population growing, the smell in those zombie-towns is almost unbearable. I don't know where the extra zombies are coming from."

Endermen hated the stench of the decaying monsters. There had been a time when an endermen's greatest joy was to clean themselves, and once they had even bathed in streams and rivers. But that had been before the Great Zombie Invasion. Now, water was poison to them, burning their skin like acid. The ability to clean their bodies had been forever taken from them—a punishment following the failed zombie war.

"So you're telling me that the zombie king is gathering zombies, but they're not coming from the zombie-towns," the king said.

The enderman nodded his dark square head.

"And that there are many more zombies in the ancient zombie-towns than there should be?"

The young enderman nodded again.

"And that they are attacking nothing, just standing around in the old caverns?"

"That is correct," the dark creature replied.

"Curious," the endermen king said as he went over this puzzling news in his head.

Eventually, Feyd let out an ear-piercing screech that cut through the silence of the End like a needle through soft flesh. The remaining endermen instantly peered in his direction, then teleported to him. Their dark bodies materialized around him, some with an instant coating of purple mist, some with delayed lavender particles. The monsters stared at each other nervously, waiting for instructions from their leader.

"Brothers and sisters, the zombies are up to something and we must know what," Feyd said in a high-pitched voice. "They are amassing a huge army and we need to know why. Their target must be identified so that the endermen can be on hand to ensure their victory. Without our teleportation powers, the zombies are useless.

"We need information. I order all of you go to the Overworld. Stay in the shadows, watch and listen," the king of the endermen commanded. "Bring back everything you learn to me. I am sure the User-that-is-not-a-user is somehow involved, and the endermen have a score to settle with him. If we can keep an eye on the zombies and get even with Gameknight999 at the same time . . . then all the better." Feyd's eyes began to glow white as the mention of his enemy's name brought forth a rage from deep within him. "NOW GO!"

The dark creatures disappeared from sight, some in a puff of purple. For others, the violet clouds only appeared moments after the monster had already vanished.

Strange . . . it's almost like Minecraft is having a hard time keeping up with us, like it's lagging behind, Feyd thought. He shrugged, then he, too, disappeared from the End in search of information about the zombies and in search of his enemy, Gameknight999.

CHAPTER 14
ENEMY SIGHTED

Xa-Tul paced back and forth in front of his commanders. Before the terrified zombies lay a pile of gold armor, three glowing balls of XP, and a pile of zombie flesh. The zombie king put away his massive broadsword, then stepped forward and allowed the XP to flow into his body.

"Xa-Tul told all the zombie generals that this was a staging area, and that attacking the villagers was not part of the plan," the king of the zombies said. "Were those instructions that difficult to understand?"

The gold-clad zombie looked down at the armor that floated on the ground. It was the only thing that remained of the zombie general who had ordered the attack.

"WAS THAT DIFFICULT TO UNDERSTAND?!" Xa-Tul yelled.

The monsters shook their head vigorously, their gazes cast to the ground.

"The purpose of bringing all these zombies to this server was not to fight with the NPCs and reduce the size of the army here," the zombie king growled. "Herobrine gave Xa-Tul a command before he left Minecraft. And to follow through on that command, all zombies must be brought to this server. Having them killed in pointless battles makes it hard for Xa-Tul to carry out Herobrine's final wishes."

He took a step forward, then stomped his massive clawed foot down on the gold chest plate that floated before him. The metal crunched and folded under his weight, as if it were made of paper. The monster glanced down at the destroyed armor, then shifted his gaze to the surviving commanders.

"Do the generals understand their commands?" Xa-Tul growled, then drew his golden broadsword. "Or must they be explained again?"

"They are understood," the generals all said quickly in unison.

"Good," the zombie king replied. "Now that the NPCs know where the zombies are hiding, it is necessary to move. Take all zombies through the green portal and to the next ancient zombie-town. That was their end destination anyway. Perhaps the final gathering will happen sooner than expected."

The generals all nodded their decaying heads.

"Now go and clear all zombies from this zombie-town," Xa-Tul commanded.

The generals shuffled quickly away, grateful to have survived the meeting. Xa-Tul watched them and sneered.

"Pathetic cowards," he growled.

Suddenly, the zombie king saw a single weak zombie stumbling across the cratered zombie-town. He struggled through the river that ran through one side, then shuffled straight toward the zombie king, screaming something at the top of his lungs.

"THE ENEMY . . . THE ENEMY!" the monster yelled.

He tripped and fell over the uneven ground, then struggled to stand again. Xa-Tul could see the zombie was exhausted, its HP nearly depleted. Rushing to his side, the zombie king grabbed the monster and threw him over his shoulder. He then moved to the HP fountain, knocking aside the other zombies with his free hand. When the green sparks of HP fell on the zombie, the monster began to breathe easier, his pale skin slowly returning to its naturally decrepit green hue.

Xa-Tul put the creature roughly on the ground, then turned him around.

"What is this about the enemy?" Xa-Tul asked. "Gameknight999 has been spotted?"

"Yes, sire," the zombie replied. "The User-that-is-not-a-user was seen during the fighting in the crevasse. This zombie saw the enemy with the two swords."

"What is this zombie's name?" Xa-Tul asked.

"Ho-Lin, Sire."

"Well done, Ho-Lin. Bringing this news to Xa-Tul has been a great service to all zombies," the king said. "Xa-Tul promotes Ho-Lin to Nu-Lin."

The zombie stood up taller, his new name increasing his rank amongst his peers.

"If Gameknight999 was here, then it is certain that they will return with an NPC army," Xa-Tul mused.

"Will the zombies wait to destroy the enemy?" Nu-Lin asked.

"No, your king has other plans," the zombie king said. "It is more imperative that the zombies leave this cave quickly."

Xa-Tul drew his massive golden broadsword, the keen edge making a terrible screeching sound as it slid from the scabbard. The noise drew the attention, and fear, of all the zombies.

"Brothers and sisters, the enemy, Gameknight999, will soon be here. A surprise is necessary to properly greet the User-that-is-not-a-user. It is time to prepare, though the battle that will crush our enemy will not happen here. Instead, Xa-Tul will draw the User-that-is-not-a-user to a place much more convenient for the zombies."

The monsters nodded their scarred heads and moaned in excitement.

"A trap will be set up in the next ancient zombie-town," Xa-Tul said, his eyes glowing bright with violent anticipation. "This time, Gameknight999 will not be underestimated. This time, it will be Xa-Tul who will be victorious."

The zombie-king laughed a malicious, evil laugh that spread through the army until the uproar filled the entire chamber.

"Quickly, remove all evidence that zombies or NPCs were here and go to the next zombie-town."

The monsters moved about the cavern and picked up all evidence, then headed for the portal chamber. Xa-Tul followed the massive monster horde down the stairs and grabbed one of his generals.

"Find a volunteer," the zombie king said.

The general quickly pointed to one of the zombies from the mob.

"What is this zombie's name?" Xa-Tul asked.

"Da-Ler, sire," the zombie replied.

"Excellent. Da-Ler has been chosen for an important assignment," Xa-Tul explained. "With this assignment comes a promotion. Da-Ler will be known as Pe-Ler."

The zombie's eyes grew wide with excitement.

"What must Da-Ler do?" the zombie inquired.

"*Pe-Ler* must stay behind and close the portal," Xa-Tul explained. "There is a captive creeper held in this chamber. The monster will be released, then Pe-Ler will attack the creature and detonate it next to the green portal. Xa-Tul does not want Gameknight999 following the zombie army to the next ancient zombie-town until the trap is prepared and ready for him. Pe-Ler will help insure victory over the enemy. Understood?"

The young zombie nodded his head eagerly.

"Excellent," Xa-Tul said.

The zombie king pulled the soon-to-be-promoted Pe-Ler aside as they waited for the zombies and their prisoners to move through the sparkling green portal. As Xa-Tul watched, he thought he saw the portal flicker momentarily, as if the shimmering green field disappeared for just an instant. But then it was back again, carrying his army to their new location.

Once the last of the zombies was through the gateway, Xa-Tul turned and faced the lone monster that remained. With his golden broadsword, the zombie king pointed to a chamber near the portal. He smashed one block, revealing a creeper, who peered out with dark black eyes. The captive monster paced back and forth in his prison cell, waiting to be released.

"Ready?" Xa-Tul asked.

The zombie nodded his head.

"Keep the creeper close to the portal so that its explosion will destroy the green teleportation field," Xa-Tul said. "Understood?"

The zombie nodded again, though fear began to trickle into its dead eyes.

"Do not fear. Just step away at the last instant, and Pe-Ler will be fine," Xa-Tul said, making the lie sound convincing.

The king of the zombies swung his sword down on the remaining block of dirt. With a second hit, the cube of brown dirt shattered, releasing the creeper. The mottled green monster stepped out of the hollow, but Pe-Ler grabbed it and pulled the monster to the green gateway. Xa-Tul nodded to the monster then stepped through the portal. As his vision wavered, he could see the zombie striking the creeper over and over until it started to glow bright white.

He stepped out of the green portal on the other side just as the sound of an explosion trickled out of the glistening doorway. Suddenly, the sparkling gateway went dark.

"Pe-Ler did it," Xa-Tul said with pride in his raspy voice. "His sacrifice will help the zombies to defeat Gameknight999." He growled in appreciation of the now-destroyed monster.

He stepped out of the portal room and into the much larger zombie-town. A small hill sat at the center of the cavern, an obsidian platform resting on its peak.

All around, the zombies stared at him with uncertainty in their eyes. They needed direction. Putting away his sword, the king of the zombies strode across the cratered ground until he reached the hill. Walking up the incline, he stepped onto the obsidian platform and glared down at his subjects.

"This will be the new home of the zombies for a while," Xa-Tul growled. "Many more will join soon."

He turned and glared at his generals. "Get the pathetic villagers working. This cave must be bigger! While the NPCs dig, the zombies will prepare a surprise for the User-that-is-not-a-user."

The monster horde moaned and growled in excitement as they raised their decaying hands into the air, their razor-sharp fingernails sparkling in the light from the many HP fountains that dotted the cavern.

Xa-Tul scanned the forest of claws that had sprouted up into the air and laughed an evil, malicious laugh.

"You will not stand a chance, Gameknight999," he growled, then strode off the hill and began making preparations.

CHAPTER 15
SEARCH FOR INFORMATION

ameknight999 paced back and forth, confused. The army had made it back to the village in the savannah in record time. The wounded were healed while others repaired weapons and armor. Everyone rested through the remainder of the night and then headed back to the zombie-town at dawn. But now that they were back, the place was empty . . . not just empty, but scoured clean.

"Let's check that room they always have at the back," Hunter suggested.

Gameknight nodded and followed his friend. They ran across the uneven floor, weaving around and climbing through the numerous craters that dotted the chamber floor. A small group of warriors followed closely behind them, while the rest of the army searched the huge cavern.

When he reached the stairway that led down to the portal room, Gameknight stopped and waited while the rest of the warriors caught up. The passage was lit by a strange blue light that flickered and pulsed as if it were alive.

"OK, everyone ready?" the User-that-is-not-a-user said.

They nodded.

"Let's go!"

The NPCs, led by Gameknight999, charged down the steps. As he took the steps two-at-a-time, Gameknight drew his swords and steeled himself for battle. But to his surprise, when they rounded the corner and entered the chamber, they found it empty, just like the cavern above. Before them stood three portals; a sickly yellow one, a purple one, and a third obsidian ring, which lay empty. Beneath the third portal was evidence that an explosion had occurred next to it, including a pile of zombie flesh and a small bit of gunpowder floating at the bottom of the newly-formed crater.

Hunter went down into the depression and grabbed the gunpowder. She held it in her hand for a moment, then knelt and placed her hand on the stone.

"It's still warm," Hunter said as she stepped out of the recession. "It must have been a creeper, and it seems like it exploded recently. But why would it detonate right next to the portal?"

"Hmm . . ." Gameknight mused as he stared down into the cavity.

"They wanted to close the portal after they left so we couldn't follow them," Cobbler said from the entrance to the room.

Gameknight turned and found Crafter standing there, his bright blue eyes sparkling in the strange portal-light.

"Maybe we should go through the different zombie-towns," Digger said. "You know, like the one your sister was in? There would probably be a portal room in each of them, just like this one."

"That's a good idea," Crafter said. "We could—"

"No!" said a strong voice from the doorway, causing everyone to turn and stare.

Herder pushed his way through the crowd that was growing near the portal room entrance.

"The zombies used this ancient zombie-town for a reason," Herder said. "Maybe they're trying to hide what they're doing. These older zombie-towns are probably not on the same portal network as the newer ones. But they chose this one, with its cratered floor and single HP fountain, for a reason, and it wasn't convenience. I mean, look: there is a river running straight through it." He stepped closer to Gameknight999 and stared up into his eyes. "This terrible, inconvenient zombie-town must be a part of their plan, and that's important to remember."

"Hmmm . . ." Gameknight said as he considered his friend's words.

"I agree with Herder," Digger said, stepping forward and patting the skinny boy on the back. Herder nearly fell over, causing many of the villagers to chuckle.

"OK, if you're right, then where do we go to find the closest ancient zombie-town?" Gameknight questioned.

All eyes swiveled to Crafter, expecting some kind of response, but the young NPC was lost in thought. He paced back and forth across the portal chamber, then turned and faced the crowd of villagers.

"Where's Bookman?" he asked to the NPCs.

"Here," said a scratchy voice.

An NPC pushed through the armored bodies and stood at Crafter's side. He wore a white smock with a gray stripe running down the center. His hair matched the color of the stripe but was messed and disheveled. Gameknight thought he was possibly the oldest NPC he'd ever seen in Minecraft—besides the original Crafter, of course.

"Gameknight, Bookman is the village's librarian," Crafter explained. "You probably haven't seen him before because he is always in his library, reading books." Crafter turned and faced the librarian. "Bookman, you remember telling me about that book on the Great Zombie Invasion?"

The librarian nodded his gray head. "Hmm . . . yes . . . it said something about how Smithy of the Two-Swords defeated Herobrine's forces, and how the zombie-towns were made. They apparently used exploding creepers to expand the caves, which many believe led to the creeper king pulling his monsters out of the war. I find it fascinating that during—"

"Bookman . . . Bookman, that all sounds very interesting, and some other time I'd love to hear more about it, but right now we need you to focus," Crafter interrupted gently. "Did the book happen to mention where the old zombie-towns were located? Do you remember?"

"Hmm . . . I know the original book was badly damaged when I first read it," Bookman said. "I wrote down what I could understand, but there were many pages missing."

"All we need to know is where *one* zombie-town is located," Gameknight added.

"Hmm . . . yes . . . I do remember something," the librarian said. "There was a zombie-town near a deep ravine, or something like that . . ."

"That sounds just like the one we're in right now!" Hunter exclaimed.

"Oh . . . hmm . . . yes, of course," Bookman continued. "And then there was one near the giant waterfall, but I'm sure you all knew about that one."

"A giant waterfall?" Gameknight asked.

"Yes, yes," Bookman replied. "The waterfall was the scene of a pivotal battle during the Great Zombie Invasion. The zombies had a town hidden in the rocks behind the waterfall. The stories say that Smithy of the Two-Swords was able to feel the zombie-town's presence and led his army right to it. I'm sure villagers already know about that one. I told them all to read that book . . . quite interesting . . . quite interesting indeed."

Gameknight snapped his head to Crafter. The young boy with the ancient eyes just shrugged.

"Bookman, none of us have had a chance to read that book yet," Crafter replied. "Sorry, but you'll have to give us a quick summary."

"Oh my . . . that is unfortunate. It is quite an exciting history of the events during—"

"On second thought, maybe we can discuss the book later," Hunter interrupted. "Right now I'd say our best bet is finding that waterfall. Anyone have any ideas where it is?"

Everyone glanced about the chamber, but the room stayed silent. Gameknight sighed and was about to speak when he heard a meek voice beside him.

"I think I know where it is," Cobbler said, his voice barely a whisper.

"You do?" Gameknight exclaimed.

The boy nodded.

"Well?" Hunter probed. "Are you gonna tell us or keep it a secret?"

"Oh . . . umm . . . it's near my village," Cobbler said.

"Great!" exclaimed Crafter.

"Here's what we will do," Gameknight said. "I will go back to Cobbler's village with the bulk of the NPCs. Crafter, you go back to the village and bring the rest of the army. We'll meet back up at Cobbler's village as soon as possible. Let's go!"

The warriors stormed out of the portal chamber and back to the tunnel that led out of the zombie-town.

"You see, Cobbler," Crafter said as he veered around a crater, "it was good luck that you were here."

"Yeah, but now I'm going to lead everyone to another zombie-town that will likely be filled with hundreds of monsters," the boy said. "That doesn't seem very lucky."

Crafter sighed and glanced at the User-that-is-not-a-user. Gameknight could tell that his friend wanted him to say something reassuring to Cobbler, but he just couldn't find the right words. After all, Cobbler was probably right. Gameknight999 knew they would likely find a massive army at the waterfall zombie-town, and he would have no choice but to lead his friends in battle, again. They would almost certainly be completely outnumbered, *again*, and he would have to figure out a way to save the NPCs and stop Xa-Tul's evil plans. Glancing around at all the villagers around him, he shuddered when he thought about some of them getting hurt, or worse.

Why am I always in the position of being responsible for so many lives? Gameknight thought. *I think Cobbler is wrong. Bag luck doesn't follow him; it follows me, like a vulture.*

With a sigh, he left the zombie-town and ran through the crevasse. When he reached the tunnel, Gameknight peered back at the dark passages and shuddered. He could feel the vultures circling around his courage, getting ready to strike.

CHAPTER 16

WATERFALL

The NPC army, now three times its original size, approached the waterfall with the newly-risen sun shining down upon them. Everyone had waited at Cobbler's village while Crafter brought the rest of the army. But when he returned through the minecart network, more villagers joined their forces. Every NPC that had heard about the captured villagers was concerned and wanted to help bring them back. Now, with the additional warriors, Gameknight was starting to feel like maybe they had a chance.

"Remember, everyone: stick to the plan when we get into the zombie-town," Gameknight said as he addressed the troops. "Our goal is to locate the villagers, get them out safely, and figure out what the zombies are doing. What we *don't* want to do is get caught in the zombies' cave and have to fight it out with them. It's likely we'll still be outnumbered, and they'll have the advantage of defending their own turf. So we go in quick and quiet."

The warriors all nodded their square heads.

"Let's go," he said, then turned and headed down the hill that led to the waterfall.

As he drew closer, the roar of the falling water grew louder and louder. Looking up, Gameknight could see it coming down off a cliff high overhead. Sheer walls of stone and dirt rose up on either side, their faces far too steep to climb. Pausing for a moment, the User-that-is-not-a-user surveyed the surroundings.

"How will we get through that waterfall?" Stitcher asked. "The water looks like it's moving pretty fast."

"I have an idea," Hunter said. "Maybe we jump off the cliff and ride the waterfall on the way down, then shoot through an opening in the wall."

"But how will we know where the opening is located?" Crafter asked.

"I didn't say it was a *good* idea," she replied.

"We could swim upstream and try to swim up the waterfall," Digger suggested.

"No, that would probably scatter the army," Crafter said.

Gameknight stared at the terrain, looking for a way through the thundering waterfall. He scanned the river banks, and the sheer cliffs, and the . . .

"Wait a minute," Gameknight said.

He moved to the closest wall and looked down. A series of stone blocks were placed haphazardly along the waterline at its base. From far away, it just looked like part of the wall, but up close, he could see that it looked like a path, with pieces either missing or purposely left out to ensure it wouldn't be easily seen.

"What are you staring at?" Hunter asked. "Admiring your reflection in the water agai—ouch!"

"Be nice, or you'll get another," Stitcher said, her hand still balled into a fist.

Gameknight didn't pay them any mind; his thoughts were still focused on the blocks before him. He stepped out onto one, then the next, and the next. With a careful leap, he flew over an exposed section, landing deftly on the block on the other side of the gap.

Glancing over his shoulder, Gameknight found the others following him, suddenly noticing the camouflaged path in front of them. Giving them a nod, he continued working his away across until he was inches away from the falling torrent of water.

"What now?" Hunter asked.

"I think we need to go through," Gameknight replied.

"Are you sure the path continues?" she asked.

"I'm not sure of anything, but if we're going to get the villagers back, we have no choice," the User-that-is-not-a-user said. "If I make it through, I'll shoot an arrow out and you'll know it's safe."

"Better you testing this out than me," Hunter said sarcastically, but gave him a concerned look.

He flashed her a smile, held his breath, and stepped into the watery flow. Instantly, his vision was filled with blue. The narrow ledge continued along the edge of the sheer wall, and after three blocks, he was out of the water and found himself in a dark cave.

Standing motionless, Gameknight listened for monsters, but the only sound was the roar of the waterfall. He placed a torch on the ground, lighting up the opening. Before him was a massive tunnel burrowing its way into the mountain, angling downward into darkness.

Pulling out his bow, he notched an arrow and fired it through the water. He could barely see it as it passed through the liquid. A moment later, Hunter stepped through with the rest of the army following close behind.

"It looks like you survived after all," Hunter said with a smile.

"Yep," Gameknight replied, then turned and faced the cavernous opening.

He could just imagine the monsters that were down there, hiding in the shadows. It made him shudder, but he gathered his courage and took a step forward into the passage.

"Come on, everyone," the User-that-is-not-a-user said as he walked. "Let's do this as quietly as possible. Remember, our goal is to save the villagers, not to start a massive battle."

The army followed him into the darkness. His enchanted armor cast enough light for him to see the ground just a few blocks ahead. Someone toward the rear placed a torch on the wall, casting a yellow circle of light on the ground, but Gameknight, being in the front, quickly walked out of the glowing patch and into darkness again.

As they progressed, they passed multiple tunnels that intersected and went off in different directions. At each one, Gameknight would stop for a moment and have one of the wolves investigate. If they caught the scent of zombie, Gameknight would hear a soft growl. If there was no scent, the wolf quickly returned. It was slow going, but they needed to make sure they were still on the right path.

"I wish we still had that zombie with us from the crevasse," Stitcher said. "It could probably have led us right where we needed to go."

"Yeah, but maybe it would have led us into a trap," Hunter added.

"Hunter is right," Crafter added. "I'm not certain the zombie led us to the crevasse because it was afraid. I think it was trying to trick us. There is something going on here that we still don't understand."

"Well, I understand what's happening," Cobbler said. "It was my bad luck that made the zombies attack my village, and look at me now. I'm wet, and my family and friends are missing, and I'm all alone; I have no one."

The shoemaker sighed and lowered his head.

"You need to look around you, Cobbler," Digger said. "You aren't alone. You're completely surrounded by friends and people who care about you."

"Well . . . my village *was* destroyed. If I didn't have bad luck, I wouldn't have any luck at all."

"You think you're unlucky?" Hunter snapped, her voice becoming agitated. "You survived an attack that captured or destroyed your entire village. I'd say that was pretty lucky."

"Cobbler, you are a bright boy and seem like you have a good block on your shoulders," Crafter said. "But as I've said to others recently—" he glanced at the User-that-is-not-a-user "—we can control how we feel by what we think. I guarantee you, if you keep on with the negative talk, then it will only make you depressed and make it more difficult for you to succeed. On the other hand, if you adopt a positive attitude and actively force yourself to say something about the good around you, then you'll be happier and feel braver. Now, which one of those things do you think will help you the most: being depressed, or being happy and brave?"

"I don't know," Cobbler mumbled as he looked sheepishly at the ground.

Hunter walked up behind the boy and banged her bow on the top of his iron helmet. It rang out like a gong, causing the boy to snap out of his funk.

"Wake up and use your head," she said firmly. "A wise NPC is telling you something important." She leaned in close and whispered in his ear. "Listen to him, or I'll bonk you on the head again."

Cobbler glared at her, then turned and faced Crafter.

"I guess being happy and brave *would* help more," the young NPC said in a meek voice.

"You don't need to convince me, Cobbler. You need to convince yourself," Crafter said, glancing at Gameknight with an inquisitive look, his eyes locked on the User-that-is-not-a-user. "Positive thoughts will drive you to success, but negative ones will only cause your ruin. You understand?"

Gameknight felt like he was expected to speak up, but before he could say anything, Cobbler replied.

"I get it, Crafter, I really do. It's just that it can be hard sometimes."

"No one said this is easy," Crafter said. "But it is a choice, and it's all up to you. Think of your life as a boat traveling on a journey, and you are the captain of the ship. You get to steer it anywhere you want. You can go toward the beautiful sunset, or you can go over a cliff . . . it's your choice. You are the captain of the boat: the boat of your life." He stepped up to Cobbler and spoke in his ear, just loud enough for Gameknight999 to hear. "Choose," he said, then glanced at the User-that-is-not-a-user one more time.

Gameknight nodded, then stared down into the dark passage. He knew Crafter was talking to him just as much as he was to Cobbler. Deep down in his soul, he knew that it was all true, but sometimes Gameknight had a hard time believing it.

It's difficult staying positive when so many negative things happen, Gameknight thought bitterly.

Suddenly, something white and furry darted past him, then another and another. Gameknight glanced over his shoulder and saw Herder looking at him, a huge smile on the young boy's face.

"They will scout ahead," the lanky boy said.

Gameknight nodded, then continued forward. With the wolves out in front, he felt more comfortable moving faster. Shifting from a walk to a run, he moved through the large tunnel as it sloped downward, going deeper and deeper underground. Occasionally, they came upon water that flowed across the tunnel. These tiny streams were quickly plugged with a block of cobblestone or dirt. But when they came across flows of lava, Gameknight999 had to be very careful. Swimming in lava was never a good idea in Minecraft.

Suddenly, a whimpering sound echoed off the walls in front of them and filled the passage. Gameknight cast Herder a glance, and the young boy smiled.

"Sounds like they found them," Herder said.

With a torch outstretched before him, the User-that-is-not-a-user sprinted through the passage. The whimpering sound became louder and louder as he neared. Soon, the wolves materialized out of the darkness as the circle of light from his torch bathed their white bodies. The animals were all facing to the side, looking straight at the wall of the tunnel, each of their tails sticking straight out. One of them glanced at Gameknight999, and he could see its eyes were blood-red; the wolves were angry and ready for battle.

Moving up to the wall, he placed the torch on the ground. It threw yellow rays of light in all directions, illuminating what was before him. Gameknight could see the material was cobblestone instead of stone, like someone had been here before. Stepping up to the wall, he placed his ear against the stone, but couldn't hear anything from the other side. Turning, the User-that-is-not-a-user glanced at Digger and nodded his square head.

The big NPC stepped forward with his pickaxe in his hands. With three quick swings, he shattered the block of cobblestone, then crushed the one beneath it. A stale smell wafted out from the hole he'd created, as if it had been trapped on the other side for a long, long time. Instantly, the wolves began to growl as the scent hit their nostrils.

"Zombies," Herder whispered, recognizing it.

Gameknight nodded in agreement.

"Everyone ready?" he asked.

The villagers all nodded, and while their eyes were filled with uncertainty and fear, the looks on their faces said they all had faith in his ability to see them through the battle.

I wish I had that much faith in myself, Gameknight thought, then stepped into the tunnel.

CHAPTER 17

HERDER

Gameknight ran through the dark passage, letting the iridescent glow of his enchanted armor light the way. With his diamond sword in his right hand and iron sword in his left, he charged forward, ready for battle. Fear pulsed through his veins with every heartbeat.

I wonder if the legendary Smithy of the Two-Swords had ever visited this *ancient zombie-town during the Great Zombie Invasion,* Gameknight thought for some reason. But then the smell of decaying flesh assaulted his nostrils and focused his attention back to the moment. How many zombies would they find ahead? Were the villager captives still alive? What was Xa-Tul up to? These questions and many more echoed through his mind as he progressed.

Suddenly, the tunnel opened up into the massive cavern that made up this ancient zombie-town. It was a gigantic cave whose width likely exceeded a hundred blocks, with a ceiling that was probably thirty blocks high, if not more. At the center of the cavern was a hill that rose a dozen blocks into the air. A dark obsidian platform sat on the top of the mound. The floor of the chamber was covered with craters, like a scene from a World War I movie. Gameknight felt as if he was about to step into no-man's land.

All along the perimeter of the cavern were tunnel entrances, all of them leading out to unknown places. Each one looked dark and empty, as if they hadn't been used in centuries.

The cavern was lit with a faint green glow: light from the many sparkling HP fountains that dotted the cavern floor. It gave the area a sort of alien appearance.

The cavern was completely silent, save the few bats that flittered and squeaked along the rocky ceiling. In fact, it was so quiet that Gameknight could hear the splash of the HP fountains; they sounded like someone sprinkling the tiniest of gems on a piece of glass. The sound was soothing, but the silence of the cavern was not. It reminded Gameknight of that moment just before the big drop on a roller coaster. He realized he was accidentally holding his breath, and slowly exhaled.

"Where are all the zombies?" Stitcher asked.

"Maybe they heard we were coming and ran away," Hunter said, sarcastically.

"Not likely," Digger replied.

"We need to look for clues," Gameknight said. "Break up into three groups. I'll lead one straight ahead. Digger will take the second group to the right, Crafter to the left. Everyone keep your eyes open. If you find anything, let the others know. We meet back here in five minutes. Go!"

Gameknight ran forward, then jumped into the bottom of a crater and quickly climbed up the other side. As he ran, he glanced around him. He could see Crafter and Hunter leading a large group along the perimeter of the cave, while Digger and Stitcher led another group to the right. Periodically, they disappeared as they moved down into one of the many craters that covered the floor.

Suddenly, he felt something brush past him. Herder appeared by his side as his wolves ran forward to scout the top of that obsidian-capped hill.

"Don't worry, Gameknight," the lanky boy said. "We'll find the villagers. I have faith in you."

Gameknight reached the top of the hill and stood on the obsidian platform. Before him, he could see the tunnel that led to the portal room. It glowed with a strange flickering radiance that seemed to shift back and forth from green to purple to a sickly yellow. He was surprised there were no zombies guarding the entrance. They had gone out of their way to destroy the green portal in the last ancient zombie-town, yet they left this one unguarded. It made no sense.

"Gameknight . . . over here!" Crafter shouted.

"Go check out the portal room, but keep your eyes peeled for danger," the User-that-is-not-a-user said to Herder and the other warriors.

Herder nodded his head, his long black hair falling across his square face. He wiped the strands away, then flashed him a smile.

"Wolves . . . forward," he said in a commanding voice, then ran down the hill to the portal room, the rest of the warriors following close behind.

Gameknight watched them leave and felt a sense of pride watching Herder. The boy had grown so much since he had first met him that night when the warriors had been bullying him. Now, he was leading a group of warriors across a zombie-town with confidence and strength. Gameknight sometimes wished he had half of the boy's courage.

Turning, the User-that-is-not-a-user sprinted down the hill and around the many craters that covered the ground until he reached Crafter's side.

"Look," the young leader said.

Gameknight stared down and saw a pickaxe floating on the ground in front of them, but nothing else.

"You think this was someone's inventory, and they died here?" Hunter asked.

"No, there would have been other items here if that happened," Crafter said.

"This was left on purpose, as a signal to us," Gameknight said.

"Or maybe a warning," Hunter added.

"And look at the ground in this tunnel over here," Crafter said.

He pulled out a torch and moved to a passageway that pierced the side of the huge cavern. Kneeling, he placed his torch on the ground and examined the stone floor.

"You see these scratches?" Crafter asked.

Gameknight knelt and peered at the ground. He could see tiny marks across the faces of the stone blocks.

"Something with claws on their feet walked across this stone, recently," Crafter said. "Notice there is no dust in the tiny crevasses."

"Zombies," Gameknight999 hissed.

Crafter nodded his head, then stood.

"They were here recently," the young NPC said.

"So where are they now?" Hunter asked.

Suddenly, a loud sorrowful wail floated out of the tunnel before them. Terrible moans filled the chamber and echoed off the stone walls over and over, making it sound like it was coming at them from all sides. Soon it became clear that angry zombie-growls were coming out of another tunnel. Then another sounded with the scratching of claws against stone.

Finally, as if on command, all the tunnels were filled with zombie moans, and they seemed to be growing louder. The smell of decaying flesh grew more intense and hit them all. It was overwhelming and made Gameknight gag. They stepped back from the opening as the moaning growls continued to increase in volume.

Then the first of the monsters emerged from a tunnel near the portal room. It was a huge zombie that jingled like the sound of broken glass clinking together as it stepped out from the shadows.

"The Fool has come to join us . . . how nice," a bombastic voice said, filling the chamber with thunder.

"Xa-Tul," Gameknight growled, immediately recognizing the zombie king.

Suddenly, huge numbers of zombies began to emerge from every tunnel, a hundred from each dark passage.

"IT'S A TRAP!" the User-that-is-a-user yelled. "Everyone, back the way we came in."

Zombies charged out of the tunnel before them, their angry growls filling the air. Gameknight sprang forward and attacked. His dual swords were a blur as he threw himself into battle, his body moving purely by instinct, without thought or fear. Many monsters succumbed to his rage as he fought, but the passage was just too wide for him to stop the overwhelming flow of the mob. Zombies slipped past him and tried to attack from behind.

Crafter, leading a set of troops, surged forward and blocked the passage in response. Those that had slipped behind Gameknight were overtaken and quickly destroyed.

"Gameknight, we need to get out of here," Crafter said. "All of the tunnels are flooded with zombies. We have to get back to the entrance before we're all trapped in this zombie-town."

But Gameknight couldn't hear; he was lost in the heat of battle. Slashing with his iron sword, he destroyed a monster on his left, then quickly shifted his attack to the monster on his right. Moving from zombie to zombie, the User-that-is-not-a-user had turned into a whirling machine of destruction.

Suddenly, something thumped him on the back of the head. Turning, he found Hunter standing there with her bow held high, ready to whack him again.

"We need to get out of here, you idiot," she said. "Now quit playing with your zombie friends and RUN!"

She reached out and pulled him away from the monsters, pushing him across the zombie-town, toward the tunnel they had used to enter the cavern. Thankfully, there were no monsters coming out of that passage, but the ones closest to it had realized it was the NPCs' only chance of escape and were now trying to cut them off. Hunter and Stitcher's flaming arrows streaked through the air and struck the green monsters.

Strangely, the flaming arrows stuck out of their bodies for a moment, then, only after a few seconds, the zombies flashed red with damage, and finally caught fire. *They should have instantly gone up in flames*, Gameknight thought as he watched.

Why was there a delay? More warriors pulled out their bows and added their arrows to the sisters' attack, everyone still running back toward the exit. Many other NPCs had noticed the delay their weapons had in causing damage as well. It was as if the Minecraft server couldn't keep up.

As he ran, Gameknight suddenly realized they didn't have everyone with them that they'd come with. Herder! He turned around to look back at the warriors that had gone on to investigate the portal room. He spotted Herder, warriors, and wolves, climbing the hill at the center of the chamber. The zombies, directed by their king, were flowing into the cavern and circling the hill, cutting those NPCs off from the rest of the army.

Gameknight could see Herder standing on the obsidian platform that sat atop the central hill, looking toward his friend with sad eyes. His wolves formed a protective ring around the villagers, but even with his "friends," the warriors had no chance of victory. They were outnumbered fifty-to-one.

The User-that-is-not-a-user charged back toward Herder. But before he had taken more than a few steps, a strong hand grabbed the back of his chest plate and pulled him to a halt.

"Gameknight, there's nothing we can do," Digger said in a solemn voice. "They're surrounded by maybe five hundred monsters, not to mention Xa-Tul. If you go out there and try to save them, you'll be killed." Digger turned him around and stared into Gameknight's eyes. "Listen to me. We cannot save them. We have to leave now."

"But it's Herder . . . my friend," Gameknight said, pleading.

"I know, but he knows we can't help him," Hunter said. "We have to focus on the people we *can* save, not the ones we can't. Now get it together and help us get out of here."

"Gameknight, we must get back to the tunnel and get out of here before we are all caught," Crafter said. "Come on."

The User that-is-not-a-user looked one last time toward the top of the hill. The NPCs were now completely surrounded, with the zombies getting closer and closer. Many of the warriors had already dropped their weapons, realizing their fate was sealed. With tears streaming down his face, Gameknight999 knew that his friends were right. With sorrow in his heart, he turned and fled.

CHAPTER 18

BATTLE TO THE SURFACE

Gameknight charged toward the exit, his eyes stinging as tears blurred his vision. Spinning like a dual-bladed pinwheel, he carved his way through the monsters that were trying to cut them off from their escape route. But every time he destroyed one zombie, two more quickly stepped up to take its place. They were coming at them from all sides, and there were too many of them.

As he fought, he glanced about the cavern and was shocked to see the floor of the chamber nearly covered with green monsters. Pain erupted along his arm. Spinning, Gameknight slashed at a monster just as a flaming arrow struck the creature in the shoulder. Gameknight continued to hit the creature with his swords, but it didn't seem to take damage . . . it just stood there. And then, after a delay, it was suddenly gone, disappearing with a *pop*.

What the heck was that? he thought.

Jumping over a crater, Gameknight finally reached the tunnel entrance, slashing and chopping at a few zombies directly in his path, keeping the monsters away from their escape route. Digger popped up at his side, smashing the creatures with his dual pickaxes. Hunter joined them, quickly placing two blocks under her to gave her a height advantage. She then fired down upon the creatures, protecting the NPCs who were most in need of her help. Stitcher then followed suit on the other side of the opening, her arrows adding to the storm of barbed rain coming from her sister.

As a result, more of the villagers were able to make it to the entrance and help set up a defense. Some were placing blocks of cobblestone on the ground as a makeshift wall to keep the monsters back, as others fired their bows into decaying bodies. Every arrow seemed to strike, but the damage increasingly seemed to arrive later than it should have, giving the monsters the opportunity for one final attack before their HP was extinguished.

"Hurry, everyone behind the barricade!" Gameknight shouted.

He ran out and pushed his way through the crowd of monsters, placing blocks of stone and dirt around the opening, creating a wider defensive wall. Some of the villagers were now climbing on top of the makeshift fortification, firing down upon the monster horde. There were so many monsters charging toward them now, they simply could not miss.

"I hope we don't run out of arrows," Stitcher said. "There are too many monsters here to take care of with bows."

Gameknight shoved a monster aside as he slashed out with his diamond blade. He ran back behind the stone wall and sealed it behind him. They could now hear the zombie's claws scratching away at their defenses. Blocks of dirt shattered under the onslaught, but hopefully the stone would last a little longer.

"Conserve your ammunition!" Gameknight shouted. "We won't stop them with just those arrows."

He then peered up at the cave wall above the tunnel entrance and smiled. Blocks and blocks of gravel sat just above the entrance. With some carefully-placed TNT, they'd be able to bring the whole roof down onto the opening.

"Everyone get ready to retreat," Gameknight shouted.

"But our friends are still out there!" someone shouted.

"We can't help them now," Gameknight forced himself to reply, the words catching in his throat like poison.

Gameknight scanned the sea of faces until he found the one he needed. "Crafter!" he shouted.

The young NPC turned and looked at the User-that-is-not-a-user. Gameknight pointed up at the gravel-laden ceiling and walls.

"Remember what your Great Uncle Weaver taught you?" he asked.

Crafter nodded his head.

Gameknight placed a cube of stone under him, then positioned a block of TNT in a hole in the wall. Crafter worked on the other side of the passage, placing blocks of TNT where they could do the most damage. Digger started carving holes in the ground with his pickaxe, filling each with the red-and-white striped cubes. From this height, Gameknight could see Herder and the other villagers surrounded by zombies. Slowly, the monsters were moving closer to the ring of wolves that surrounded the NPCs. The User-that-is-not-a-user knew the animals would not last long under all those zombie claws.

Herder looked across the chamber at the User-that-is-not-a-user and waved one last time, then said something to the wolves. The animals gave off a sorrowful howl, then ran from the hill and headed toward the escape tunnel. Gameknight knew that Herder had just saved the animals' lives, but the majestic wolves did not look happy about it.

Without the ring of fangs, the zombies moved up to the captured villagers and grabbed weapons from blocky hands. Xa-Tul then stepped onto the platform and grabbed Herder by the scruff of the neck. The zombie king pulled him off the obsidian platform on which he was standing and dragged him off the hill.

"Gameknight . . . " Herder wailed, then became silent.

Suddenly, a wave of furry white shapes jumped over the barricade and into the tunnel. Herder's wolves darted into the tunnel, with the pack leader moving to Gameknight's side. They growled at the zombies that were trying to claw their way through the stone wall, their fur sticking straight up. A block shattered. Cracks appeared on another, then shattered into dust. More blocks began to fail as the zombies pushed forward.

"We have to get out of here . . . now!" Digger shouted. "Everyone, back into the tunnel."

The villagers left the wall and ran up into the passageway, Stitcher in the lead. Gameknight backed up to the blocks of TNT, then pulled out flint and steel. Hunter solemnly watched as he made his preparations.

"You ready?" she asked.

Gameknight nodded his head. She pulled out her own flint and steel.

"Now!" she said, then set the explosive blocks to blinking. Gameknight did the same.

"Let's get out of here, quick!" she cried and raced up the sloping ground into the darkness of the tunnel.

"Come on!" she shouted, her voice already fading in the distance.

Gameknight backed away, glancing toward the NPC prisoners being ushered off the hill. He felt helpless, unable to do anything for them. He couldn't avoid feeling like he was abandoning them all. Reluctantly, he began to turn and join the rest of the NPCs up the tunnel.

But suddenly, to his shock, a group of endermen appeared out of nowhere on the opposite side of the zombie-town. At least twenty of them materialized in a sputtering purple mist, as well as a single dark red one, the color of dried blood. It was Feyd, the king of the endermen. Gameknight's throat went dry with fear; his limbs were frozen, like he no longer had control over his own body. He brought his eyes slowly back to the cobblestone barrier just as the remaining blocks holding the zombies back shattered, and the monsters finally broke through the defenses.

Gameknight grimaced, then suddenly remembered the blocks of TNT they'd set to explode. The cubes were blinking faster and faster . . . they were about to go off! Feeling returned to his limbs. He'd waited too long, and was too close to the impending blast radius. The cubes had turned bright white, and there was nothing Gameknight could do but close his eyes and wait to suffer the consequences of his fatal mistake.

But the cubes did not explode, when they clearly should have. It was as if the TNT was delayed, just like when the zombies took longer for their XP to expire!

Whatever was causing these glitches in Minecraft, luck was on Gameknight's side. The monsters continued to pour over what was left of the barricade, towards the tunnel. He turned and ran as fast as he could, away from the zombie horde as their clawed feet clicked on the hard stone ground. After Gameknight had sprinted a half-dozen blocks, an explosion shook the walls around him as a blast of heat pushed him forward. Gravel began to fall from the walls and ceiling as the tunnel collapsed. The detonations continued, echoing for a moment or two until the tunnel behind him finally became quiet.

Gameknight turned to look back where he'd come from, well aware of how close he'd come to being destroyed. All he saw was a huge mountain of gravel. The monsters had been caught in the blast and avalanche; the tunnel was sealed, and Herder and the other NPCs were gone.

Gameknight sat down on the ground and began to weep.

"Herder . . ." he moaned. "All those NPCs, taken prisoner because of me."

He shook as his sobs of grief and guilt filled the tunnel.

"Gameknight, we have to go," Crafter said into his ear. "It's important to mourn those we lost, but we have to keep moving or we'll all meet the same fate."

He glanced up into Crafter's bright blue eyes and nodded.

"You're right," Gameknight said as he stood.

Turning, he walked up through the passage with his head hung low.

I caused the loss of all those villagers . . . and Herder, one of my dearest friends, Gameknight thought. *I can't do any good in Minecraft. This proves that I'm a failure.*

And as he wept, the User-that-is-not-a-user followed those in front of him, his mind numb to the outside world. He didn't see anything, or hear, or even know where he was. All he could feel were the waves of grief and guilt that smashed down upon his soul.

"Herder, I've failed you again," Gameknight mumbled as he stumbled through the tunnel.

CHAPTER 19

THE MONSTER KINGS MEET

Feyd stood in the shadows and watched as the zombie king ushered the prisoners back down into the portal room. The Endermen were off to the side, far away from any of the fighting. Feyd glanced at a ledge perched high up on the cavern wall. His teleportation powers sputtered for just an instant, then he materialized on the outcropping and looked down to survey the scene below. His endermen appeared at his side and stared down with him at the decaying green monsters.

"Move faster!" Xa-Tul bellowed from across the cavern. "All zombies must leave this zombie-town. The User-that-is-not-a-user now knows of this location as well and will be back with more forces. The zombies must be gone before they arrive."

"Why are the zombies afraid of the villagers?" one of Feyd's commanders asked in a soft, screechy voice. "They have five hundred zombies here, maybe more. The villagers could never defeat that many. Are they just going to run away every time Gameknight999 finds them?"

"I don't know," growled the king of the endermen. "There is something going on here that I do not understand, and that makes me mad."

The dark red leader glanced at the twenty endermen there with him, then turned and glared back at the zombie king.

"Endermen . . . with me."

He disappeared in a cloud of purple mist, then reappeared directly in front of Xa-Tul. It took a moment for the teleportation particles to appear, but after a second, he was surrounded by the energized particles.

"Xa-Tul did not order the endermen to come here," the zombie king grumbled. "None of your kind are wanted. Or needed."

"I saw your battle with the villagers. That was impressive," Feyd said.

The zombie king stopped for a moment, then beamed with pride as the words reached the ears of his subordinates.

"Those NPCs didn't stand a chance against you and your forces," the dark monster continued. "It was a well-executed plan and now you have all these prisoners. What will you do with them?"

It made him slightly sick to his stomach to pretend to flatter a giant oaf like Xa-Tul, but Feyd knew he could get the zombie king talking just by appealing to his overinflated ego. Giving him a few compliments in front of his subordinates would surely loosen his tongue.

"The king of the endermen likes Xa-Tul's plan?" the zombie king inquired. "It is not surprising, given how great of a king and warrior Xa-Tul is. Xa-Tul knew Gameknight999 was coming and made sure he felt the sting of my warriors' claws."

And yet you let him get away, you idiot, Feyd thought.

"You are quite right, as usual. But tell me, Xa-Tul, what will you do with the prisoners?" he queried.

The zombie king chuckled; it sounded like something between a laugh and a moan.

"They will dig for me," Xa-Tul said. "We must make room for more zombies, and these villagers will be happy to help out the zombie king . . . if they wish to live."

He laughed again, this time louder. Feyd could see the prisoners cringe, all except one. A tall, skinny villager seemed to stand tall and brave. He was facing away from their conversation, but Feyd could tell he was listening in. No matter, he would never escape to give away anything he heard. Villagers were quite pathetic creatures, especially when they didn't have the User-that-is-not-a-user to lead them.

Feyd was about to ask another question and draw some more information from the foolish zombie king when Xa-Tul abruptly turned away and headed down the flight of stairs that led to the portal chamber. Feyd followed close behind, his own dark warriors right on his heels. The endermen king wanted to see what was happening. When he reached the small room, he found three tall obsidian rings, each sparkling with a different color of light. The zombies were moving in a single file to the green portal, traveling to the next ancient zombie-town.

"Xa-Tul, why are you abandoning this chamber and using the portal to go to another zombie village?" Feyd asked. "Surely there is room enough for your great zombie army, which is probably one of the greatest armies ever seen in Minecraft." The fake compliment almost made him gag.

The endermen moved next to their king, their hands already balled into fists, unable to help being irritated at hearing such lavish praise for the zombies.

"The zombies cannot stay here," the zombie king said. "The User-that-is-not-a-user will certainly return with more NPCs."

"But look around you. Easily you have enough zombies to repel any attack they could mount. You are safe here. It is possible to stay and fight."

"Fighting is not the plan," Xa-Tul said.

"What?" Feyd exclaimed. "Since when do zombies run from a fight?"

"Xa-Tul is obeying the Maker's last command," the zombie said proudly. "Herobrine gave specific instructions to Xa-Tul before leaving this world, and the zombies will see it done."

"He did, did he? What were his instructions?" the king of the endermen probed as zombies rushed past him and piled into the sparkling green portal. *Why would Herobrine ever entrust his last command to a dumb zombie like Xa-Tul?* Feyd wondered bitterly. The thought alone made him jealous; he'd always thought he was Herobrine's favorite monster king.

"Herobrine's instructions were for the zombies to carry out, not the endermen," Xa-Tul said. "Everything the enderman king does seems to end in disaster. Xa-Tul will not allow Feyd to mess this up. This task is for the zombies and *only* the zombies."

"You fool, if Herobrine gave you a command, then it was meant for *all* monsters," Feyd said, lying through his teeth, trying to outsmart him.

The zombie king growled at the insult. Drawing his huge golden broadsword, he turned to face the endermen. The hundreds of zombies around him sensed their king's rage and extended their claws towards the endermen.

"The enderman king will no longer talk to Xa-Tul with disrespect," the zombie king said. "Look around. Does Feyd think it is possible to defeat a hundred zombies? Xa-Tul just needs to command it and the endermen in this chamber will be destroyed."

The endermen around Feyd drew on their teleportation powers, but the purple particles did not come right away; they seemed to sputter and flicker like a torch that was slowly burning out. Xa-Tul laughed, his bellowing voice echoing off the stone walls.

"Come, zombies," Xa-Tul boomed. "Leave these fools to stand here in the darkness. Our true destination lies elsewhere."

The monsters drew in their claws and backed away from the endermen. They continued their orderly parade into the portal until the last of them had vanished, leaving just Xa-Tul behind to face the endermen. Carefully, he slid his broadsword into its scabbard, then stared at the endermen king.

"With the numbers of zombies in my army, there is no need for the endermen. If Feyd and his puny endermen get in Xa-Tul's way, the zombies are strong enough to destroy all endermen, regardless of the teleportation powers the endermen possess. The enderman king can help in this endeavor, or get out of the way. Those are the only choices. But make no mistake, Xa-Tul is in command, and any disrespect or disobedience will have fatal consequences. Feyd must choose to help the zombies, or disappear back to that pathetic floating island in the End."

The zombie king stared at Feyd, his tiny eyes glowing red with anger and determination. But just as Feyd was about to answer him, the zombie king stepped through the portal and disappeared, traveling to the next zombie-town, leaving the endermen alone in the room.

"What is his plan?" Feyd said to himself as he turned away from the portal. "He will surely mess this up somehow, and it will be left to the endermen to clean up their failure, as always."

If only endermen could use that green portal, then we could just follow the zombies, Feyd thought. *But those gateways will not work for our kind.*

He turned and faced his warriors.

"Find which zombie-town they went to . . . hurry!"

The dark creatures disappeared one after the other until only Feyd was left, alone with the sparkling portals.

"What are you up to, Xa-Tul?" the king of the endermen said to the empty chamber. "Make no mistake about it, I will find out. And when you mess this up, the king of the endermen will be there to snatch victory from your hands. And then I will make you suffer, Xa-Tul, for not including me in the first place."

He cackled a spine-cringing laugh, then disappeared in a cloud of sputtering, flickering, inconsistent purple mist.

CHAPTER 20

FINDING COURAGE

The minecart clattered on the metal rails as it shot through the dark tunnel. Ahead, Gameknight could just barely make out Hunter's curly red hair as she faded in and out of view. And then she disappeared again, racing ahead, making him feel as if he were the only person in the tunnel.

The darkness wrapped around him like an ice-cold blanket of guilt as he thought about his friend Herder. In the minecart behind him was Herder's wolf, the pack leader. Its minecart was nearly touching Gameknight's. They were so close, he could hear the animal whine and whimper, sad to have lost their villager leader. All of the wolves knew they'd left something dear and important behind, and the animals wanted to go back and fight, but the User-that-is-not-a-user wouldn't let them. He knew it would mean the death of all the wolves, and he couldn't be responsible for yet even more tragedy.

How many times, now, had he caused the demise of others? The list of the fallen ran through his mind and it seemed endless.

"Maybe bad things just happen to me," Gameknight said to the wolf.

The animal's ears perked up when he heard the voice. The wolf turned and gazed at the User-that-is-not-a-user.

"I need to call you something . . . a name," Gameknight said as he wiped tears from his cheek. "Buck . . . I'll call you Buck from one of my favorite books, *The Call of the Wild*. That OK with you . . . Buck?"

The animal barked once in approval, then settled his head on the edge of the minecart and stared off into the darkness. Gameknight sighed and then closed his eyes. Thoughts about all the bad things that had happened to him since coming into Minecraft flooded into his mind.

Tears began to flow again. He tried to choke them back, but the loss of his friend was too overwhelming. The image of Herder standing on the block of obsidian and staring back at him, while Gameknight could do nothing to help, haunted him. His imagination ran wild at all the possible fates that the lanky boy might currently be suffering. He could be dead, or maybe being tortured for information, or . . . Gameknight forced the thoughts from his mind. Tiny cubes of tears tumbled down his cheeks again, as they had during most of the terrible flight through the minecart network.

"I failed you, Herder," Gameknight moaned. "I left you to be captured by the zombies. I should have been by your side."

His sobs echoed off the tunnel walls.

"Maybe if I'd never come into Minecraft, then Herder would still be OK!" Gameknight shouted into the darkness.

And then suddenly he was enveloped in bright light. His minecart shot out of the tunnel and rolled into the crafting chamber. Around him, Gameknight saw chaos. All of the villagers were talking at once, telling those who had stayed behind in the village what had happened in the zombie-town. Cries of grief rose above the din as loved ones learned of the loss of their husbands and wives and sons and daughters.

"This was my fault," a voice said to his right.

Gameknight turned and found Cobbler standing in the far corner, hiding in the shadows.

"That's just not true, Cobbler," Crafter said as he moved to his side. "This was no one's fault."

"Everything bad happens to me," the young boy moaned. "It's always been that way, and it's never gonna change."

Gameknight could see the boy felt guilty for the tragedy that had befallen their friends. He wanted to say something to him, to help ease his suffering, but he couldn't; he felt the same. His friends had counted on the User-that-is-not-a-user to get them safely into that zombie-town and back out again. But in Gameknight's arrogance, he thought he could handle anything that Xa-Tul threw at them. . . . He never expected he'd have to face almost a thousand zombies. He'd underestimated the zombie king and paid dearly for his error. His *friend* had paid even more dearly.

Gameknight knew exactly how Cobbler felt, he realized. How many times had he led his friends into danger and escaped, but left behind piles of weapons and armor from fallen comrades? Ever since he'd come into Minecraft, the NPCs had been under attack from Herobrine and his monster kings, but this time, he'd brought the fight to the monsters. Look at what happened as a result. No, this wasn't Cobbler's fault . . . it was his own.

The User-that-is-not-a-user sat on a block of stone, his body slumped over as if all his bones had left his body. He felt defeated.

"Cobbler, you need to understand that life is made up of a million different events," Stitcher said. "We make the best decisions we can through life, and then we deal with the consequences. Sometimes the consequences are good and sometimes they are bad. But it isn't usually that clear which is which. Often, I've found that consequences can have both good *and* bad aspects to them."

"Really?" Cobbler asked.

Stitcher nodded her head, her curly red hair bouncing like so many crimson springs.

"A while ago, our village was destroyed by monsters, and I was taken prisoner," she explained. "The evil Malacoda took me to his fortress in the Nether and made me work for him. I'd become a slave and didn't know how long I would be allowed to live. I was terrified. Lots of NPCs tried to fight back, but they were all destroyed by the ghasts and the blazes. It seemed like the end of the world for me. But then this guy showed up." Stitcher reached out and put a hand on Gameknight's shoulder. "He figured out how to defeat the monsters and save me. Before I was saved, I thought everything was terrible, but I didn't even consider that something great might be just around the corner. If I'd continued focusing on how bad everything was, I probably wouldn't have become friends with Gameknight999. But I refused to quit, and instead helped Gameknight999 continue the fight."

The User-that-is-not-a-user sat up a little taller and glanced toward Stitcher, her words of support comforting him.

The young girl stared at the User-that-is-not-a-user and gave him a smile. And in that moment, Gameknight could feel all the gratitude and affection she felt for him. She was truly grateful for knowing him, and thankful for everything he'd ever done for her. He could tell from the look in her deep brown eyes that she meant every word.

He stood and turned to face his friend.

Maybe everything that happened to me in Minecraft wasn't bad after all, the User-that-is-not-a-user thought, his friend's words giving him courage.

"And look at us now," Stitcher continued. "Because of Gameknight999, we are a part of this new village. You are too, Cobbler. Everyone around us is part of our new family." She held her arms out as if she were enveloping the entire crafting chamber in one gigantic hug. "This is one enormous family. We laugh together, and we cry together, and sometimes, we mourn together. But we are all in this together, and you are now part of that. I'd say that's a good thing."

Gameknight smiled as he listened to Stitcher's words. She was right. This *was* one huge family, and everyone would do anything to help another. None of the villagers looked at him with blame in their eyes for the loss of a loved one. In fact, they cherished the support others were giving them. The User-that-is-not-a-user finally understood that they would do anything to help those in need, even if it meant taking up arms against a massive army of zombies. They all knew the risks and were still willing to follow Gameknight999 into battle.

He stood up a little taller.

"So when you say only bad things happen to you, Cobbler," Stitcher continued, "I say you aren't searching hard enough. Good things are all around you. You just have to open your eyes." She took a step closer to the young boy and placed a hand on his shoulder. "If you want to feel good, then search for the good. Focusing on the bad only feeds all your fears and worries. But the great thing is that you get to *choose* how you want to feel. Like Crafter said, create the fate you want."

"But sometimes bad things happen," Cobbler replied. "What do you do about them?"

"I have my family to help me through the tough times," Stitcher said as she turned in a circle and gazed across the crafting chamber. "Our captured friends have each other right now. And when we are ready, we'll return to the zombie-town and get them back."

Gameknight moved closer to the young girl and put his arm around her shoulders. Her strength and courage were like a bolt of lightning in his soul. He'd missed the most important thing all along: he was surrounded by people who would help him shoulder the responsibility for this challenge. None of them blamed him for the losses in the zombie-town. In fact, many looked upon him with sympathy in their eyes, for they could see the guilt that was raking his soul.

Someone placed a muscular hand on his left shoulder and gripped him firmly. Turning his head, he saw it was Digger, his green eyes filled with compassion. And then another hand settled on his right. It was Hunter, her brown eyes brimming with confidence in him. Glancing around the chamber, the User-that-is-not-a-user realized that all the villagers were staring at him with affection and understanding. It was as if an overpowering weight of guilt was suddenly lifted in that instant, freeing his thoughts. He was not alone, and their compassion and support felt like a warm blanket, or a reassuring hug from his mom and dad.

A recent memory flashed into his head. It was of him and his dad, Monkeypants_271, playing on his Minecraft server. He hadn't been able to see it before, because of the shroud of guilt and self-pity, but now the User-that-is-not-a-user could picture it clearly. Gameknight and Monkeypants had been testing a new minigame called TNT-Defense that was just installed on their Minecraft server. He smiled when he remembered defeating his dad for the first time. Gameknight knew this was part of the solution: TNT. Somehow, they'd use it to save their friends . . . but how? Instead of a shadow of guilt shrouding his soul, he had a raging fire of anger filling him from within. Gameknight999 refused to give up!

"We aren't going to wait," the User-that-is-not-a-user suddenly growled. "We know where the zombies are, and we're going to go in there and get them."

"But you saw how many zombies were in there," Hunter said. "We can't fight that many. Even if we had three or four more villages with us, we'd still be outnumbered."

"We'll get more villagers to join us, lots more, but we won't need them all, because I have an idea that I think you'll like."

Hunter smiled.

"It's all bouncing around in this thick head of mine, but it's time to prepare. When we get to the zombie-town, I'll have it figured out. Now, it's time we got ready for war."

"Now you're talking!" Hunter exclaimed.

Gameknight smiled.

"We have a lot to do. Let's get to work," the User-that-is-not-a-user said, his voice ringing with confidence for the first time in a long time. "But first, we're going to need more warriors, and lots of TNT."

CHAPTER 21

THE PRISONER

A pair of clawed hands shoved Herder roughly through the green portal, right into the back of Bookman, the villager in front of him. But Bookman disappeared before he could make contact, the old NPC vanishing just as the lanky boy entered the sparkling green gateway. When he stepped out of the portal, Herder was stunned by the overwhelming stench of the place they'd been taken to. He looked around. The scene was like all the others, a gigantic cave filled with the aroma of decaying flesh, but like so many of the zombie-towns they'd been pushed through, none of the monsters were staying.

One thing the villagers had not known before was that there were two sparkling green portals in every zombie-town, one that led to the previous cavern and one to the next. After being captured by Xa-Tul and his mob of monsters, Herder and the prisoners had been ushered through many of these portals as they were taken from one zombie-town to the next.

In fact, there were so many that they'd lost count of the number of portals they'd stepped in and out of. But now, it looked like they'd finally arrived at their destination. The captives were shoved quickly out of the portal room and into the center of this new zombie-town. In this new cavern, Herder saw zombies everywhere. They were crowded together on one side of the town, likely so there would be room for the flow of monsters that was still coming through the shimmering green doorway.

With the huge number of stinking creatures in the cavern, it made the space feel small, but in fact, the room was the largest Herder had ever seen. The floor was pockmarked with craters, just like the other ancient zombie-towns, but some NPC captives had been ordered to use cobblestone to patch these holes, making movement across the cavern floor much easier.

On a nearby wall, Herder spotted villagers hard at work digging into the cavern wall, slowly expanding the cave, one block at a time. Herder could see they all were near complete exhaustion, but he suspected that if the NPCs stopped to rest, there would be lethal consequences. Nearby, a massive zombie stood watch, claws extended from his muscular hands, their razor-sharp tips glistening in the emerald light of the many HP fountains around them. The monster continually growled at the NPCs as they worked, shouting insults and threats.

Suddenly, a strong hand shoved Herder toward the diggers.

"Get moving, NPC," a zombie growled, pushing him along with the other prisoners.

As he walked toward his fellow villagers, Herder glanced over his shoulder at the portal room. There were so many monsters still entering. They had to be emptying out the other zombie-towns and sending every zombie in Minecraft here. Why?

"Why do you think the zombies retreated from the last zombie-town?" Herder said as quietly as he could to Bookman in front of him. "There's no way that Gameknight could return with enough warriors to defeat so many zombies."

"Shut up, villager," a zombie growled.

A clawed hand raked across Herder's back. Pain exploded as the claws dug into his flesh. He flashed red and took a bit of damage. The zombie king, Xa-Tul, had made all the villagers remove their armor when they were in the last zombie-town. Now, they had no defense against the razor-sharp claws.

"Why are they collecting all of these zombies?" whispered one of the villagers.

Herder looked to the left and saw it was Carver speaking. But before Herder could answer him, a large green fist slammed into the NPC's head.

"Be quiet," growled a big zombie nearby.

Carver nearly toppled to the floor with the force of the blow, but Herder was able to catch him before he hit the ground. If he had fallen, likely all the hundreds of clawed zombie feet that followed the group of captives would have trampled him.

"Thanks," Carver whispered in Herder's ear.

He nodded, then reached behind him to let Herder pull him back to his feet. They were then all led past the NPC diggers and ushered to a wall on the far side of the chamber.

"All prisoners, come this way, NOW!" one of the zombies barked.

Monsters poked the NPCs in the back with the sharp points of their gold swords, guiding them toward the angry voice. They were brought to a flat section of the cave. A huge zombie stood at the center of the flat section, a pile of items floating at his feet.

"This zombie's name is Ot-Kil. The villagers will refer to Ot-Kil as Master," the massive zombie said. "If a villager has a weapon, put it here. If a weapon is found on a villager, the penalty will be death."

No one moved. The NPCs exchanged nervous glances. Suddenly, Ot-Kil reached out and cuffed a baker across the back of the head. He fell to the ground in a heap.

"Perhaps an example needs to be made to motivate the villagers to cooperate," the zombie said.

He reached down, picked up a golden sword, and stepped up to Baker. As he raised the sword, Herder spoke up quickly.

"No need to make an example. Here are our weapons."

The lanky NPC reached into his inventory and pulled out an iron sword. He tossed it into the pile of weapons that floated before him. He then pulled out his bow and a stack of arrows and added them to the collection as well. Glancing at the other villagers, Herder nodded his head.

"It's OK. Give them your weapons."

Slowly, more weapons began to add to the pile as the villagers surrendered their tools of war. One of the NPCs was about to toss his pickaxe into the pile, but was stopped by the large monster.

"NO!" the zombie snapped. "Villagers will be digging. Keep all shovels and pickaxes and food. This is all that will be needed to ensure survival. Anything else, though, will receive the harshest of punishments."

The last of the weapons clattered to the ground.

"Now follow closely," the zombie said. "Those who stray too far away will likely be destroyed."

The monster turned and stormed away. Herder moved quickly forward and motioned for the others to follow.

"Come on, everyone . . . keep up and follow instructions," Herder said, hoping that everyone would do as they were told and avoid any unnecessary violence.

As they passed a dark tunnel, though, one of the villagers, a burly stone cutter, made a dash for freedom. As he ran, he drew an iron sword that he'd kept hidden in his inventory. A zombie jumped in front of him, but the sword sliced through the air before the creature could attack. The monster disappeared with a *pop,* leaving behind three glowing balls of XP. The big zombie stopped to watch the escape attempt, but surprisingly, did nothing to stop the prisoner; he just watched, an evil smile on his face.

"Go Stonecutter . . . go!" one of the NPCs yelled.

Ot-Kil moved quickly, much faster than Herder would have thought possible, knocking that NPC to the ground. He then ground his clawed foot into the villager until he moaned in pain.

"Be quiet, slave," Ot-Kil growled, then stepped away and allowed the prisoner to stand again.

Herder turned back just in time to see Stonecutter dodge past multiple zombies, then shoot into the dark tunnel. He gave a sigh of relief as the villager disappeared.

He made it, Herder thought.

But then they heard the sound of fighting in the dark passage. Shouts of anger and pain echoed out of the shadowy tunnel, until it was suddenly silent. Herder peered at Ot-Kil and noticed a satisfied smile growing on his scarred, decaying face. A gold-clad monster stepped out of the passage and moved to stand before Ot-Kil. He held Stonecutter's iron sword in his hand. The zombie smiled, then moved to a pool of lava that bubbled near a fissure in the ground and dropped the sword into the molten stone.

"That one won't be needing a sword anymore," Ot-Kil said with an evil chuckle. "NPCs who wish to stay alive . . . might not want to follow in that villager's footsteps."

Ot-Kil pushed through the massive collection of zombies, shoving aside anyone who dared get in his path. The NPCs followed closely behind. The hungry stares from the zombies around them made the villagers feel like if it weren't for Ot-Kil, they might all be goners.

As they wended their way through the cavern, Herder looked back at the tunnel they'd emerged from. Zombies of all shapes and sizes were still arriving from the portal room, each with a hungry expression on their rotting faces, but the flow was dwindling.

"Interesting," Herder muttered to himself.

Glancing to the center of the gigantic chamber, he saw a large raised platform, constructed completely out of obsidian, with cubes of gold trimming the edges. Standing atop the obsidian square stood Xa-Tul. His chain mail sparkled in the light of the nearby HP fountains, making it appear bejeweled. He wore a golden crown made of what looked like razor-sharp claws gleaming in the green light. It sat at a slight tilt on his square head, as if it might fall off at any moment.

The zombie king glared down at him with such an evil expression of contempt on his face that Herder felt compelled to turn away, for fear of being burned by the hateful glare.

"This way," Ot-Kil growled.

They headed into a brightly-lit passage, which seemed out of place in this dimly-lit cave. It stretched far into the distance, the end lost in the haze of Minecraft. Once they entered the passage, the sound of digging filled Herder's ears. All along the sides of the passage, NPCs were working furiously, expanding the passage in all directions. There were probably at least a hundred of them, all standing shoulder to shoulder as they hammered their pickaxes into the stone walls.

"Here is where the new villagers will dig," Ot-Kil said. "More space is needed for Xa-Tul's zombies. If this space is not ready when more warriors come from the next server, then NPCs will be thrown into lava to motivate the others to work harder."

The big zombie glared at the villagers, who had all stopped their digging to listen to the slave master.

"Perhaps an example is needed right now?" the zombie overseer growled. "No one said that work should stop!"

Instantly, the NPCs turned and began swinging their picks and shovels again, tearing into the stone walls with all their might.

"Now, for all newcomers: instructions are quite simple. DIG!" Ot-Kil shouted as he shoved one of the villagers toward the wall. Herder pulled out his pickaxe and found an open place where he could fit his scrawny body.

"We are doomed," the villagers whispered next to him. "We dig until we die. This is hopeless. Maybe the lava would be a merciful end."

"We are not without hope," Herder said. "The User-that-is-not-a-user will come for us, you'll see. Just have faith that things will be better and focus on that. Conserve your strength when you can. We must all be ready to fight when the time comes."

"Fight?" the NPC said. "Are you insane? Did you see all the monsters out there? There is no escape from this chamber. This will be our tomb and final resting place."

"You must have faith," Herder lectured. "Where there are friends to help you, there is always hope. My friend Gameknight999 will come for us. . . . I know it."

The sound of Gameknight's name caused some of the heads to turn toward Herder.

"He will come for us, you will see," the lanky youth promised. "But we must be ready. If we give up, then we guarantee our fate. But if we are ready to fight, we can help ourselves when the time is right."

Herder stared at the zombie guards and could see that they were at the far end of the passage, backs turned to them.

"Have faith, brothers and sisters," Herder said. "The User-that-is-not-a-user will be here as soon as he can."

A few smiles cracked through dirty faces as hope began to flicker in their eyes.

CHAPTER 22

MONSTROUS ALLIES

The king of the endermen appeared in a dim passage, a delayed cloud of purple teleportation particles appearing around his body; this glitch still greatly disturbed him.

Why would the mechanisms of Minecraft begin to slow? he thought.

A sense of dread momentarily filled his soul, making him shudder. Quickly, he glanced around to see if there were any other creatures watching him. The tunnel was dark and silent, just the way he liked it. But then he heard the quick scurrying of feet against stone. The smell of gunpowder wafted through the tunnel; a creeper was near. He stepped out of the shadows just as a creeper emerged from around the corner. Feyd let his eyes glow bright white as he stared at the green, mottled creature. It saw the enderman king and wisely retreated back into the tunnel.

Suddenly, the passage was filled with a whooshing sound as more of his subjects materialized around him. He saw the same thing as his warriors arrived: intermittent lavender clouds that sputtered and flickered, as if the mechanisms of Minecraft were somehow skipping a beat. The purple clouds of particles eventually became fully formed, allowing all of his monsters to materialize in the tunnel. When the lavender mist dissipated, the creatures blended in with the darkness, their bodies becoming shadowy specters.

"Show me the way," the king of the endermen said.

One of the shadowy creatures stepped forward and led the way through the curving tunnel. Feyd followed at the enderman's side while the other monsters fell in behind him. They followed the curving passage as it descended into the depths of Minecraft. At some places, deadly water flowed from springs or splashed down from the ceiling. At these points, the endermen slowed their pace and carefully moved around the watery hazards. All of them knew that water would burn their skin like acid. They kept their distance from the gurgling pools, teleporting past them when they could, or walking far around the dangerous puddles.

As they continued on, Feyd began to sense the faintest smell of ash and smoke, likely from a lava flow somewhere nearby. He smiled. All monsters liked lava. It felt safe and comfortable to them, for some reason, even though they were not impervious to the burning touch of the molten stone like their cousins, the blazes. But still, the smell of the smoke and ash brought a smile to Feyd's dark red face. The aroma grew stronger and stronger as they descended deeper into the labyrinth of tunnels.

Soon, they reached a small cave maybe a half-dozen blocks wide and twice that in length. On one end, lava fell from the ceiling, the boiling stone splashing to the ground then spreading out across the floor, creating an orange, glowing lake of heat.

Nearby, water poured from a hole in the wall and spread out across the cave floor in the opposite direction. Where the two met, the smoking lava and the cool water formed a shining field of obsidian. The black cubes with purple dots glowed and sparkled in the orange light.

"Is this the entrance?" Feyd asked.

The enderman nodded his head.

The wall opposite them had a flat section that seemed out of place against the rough-hewn perimeter of the cavern. Right in the center of the flat section, a single cube of stone stuck out, as if intentionally placed there. One of the endermen teleported to the wall and placed a dark hand on the stony protrusion. The monster pushed the block, then stood back and watched . . . nothing happened. He reached out and pushed it again, and again . . . nothing.

The enderman glanced at Feyd, confused. But when he raised his hand to push it again, a grinding sound filled the passage. The walls shook as dust rained down from the ceiling. The scraping noise became louder and louder, then a section of the wall began to slide back, revealing a secret passage.

"I'm sorry. It must have been delayed for some reason. . . ." the enderman said, clearly confused.

As soon as the doorway was open far enough for Feyd to see the other side, he teleported through the hidden passage, materializing at the other end at the speed of thought. What the enderman king saw shocked him.

Before him was the largest zombie-town he'd ever seen. It was massive, with the walls to the left and right lost in the haze of Minecraft. The floor was roughly carved, and the ground was uneven and pitted with small craters, though some of them were filled in with cobblestone. The ceiling was likely forty blocks high, tall enough to make even a ghast comfortable.

But almost more shocking than the size was the smell. It was terrible, a mixture of rotting flesh, stale air, and dusty floors. It made Feyd want to gag, but he could not show any such weakness in front of his own warriors.

Turning, he saw the same expression of shock on his subjects' faces.

"This is probably one of the zombie-towns from the great war," Feyd said to himself.

"What?" replied the enderman who had just materialized next to him.

"Nothing," snapped Feyd.

The massive cave was devoid of any randomly-placed houses that you would normally find in a modern zombie-town. In fact, there were no homes here at all, just a massive open space filled with more zombies than Feyd could count. At the center of the chamber stood an ornately decorated obsidian platform. It was probably four blocks across and just as many long. It stood atop pillars of gold with the shining cubes trimming the edges of the dark platform. Standing at the center of the dark platform was the zombie king himself, Xa-Tul.

Feyd turned around and looked at his warriors.

"All of you, stay here unless I signal for you," Feyd said. "Do you understand?"

The endermen nodded their dark heads.

"Stick to the shadows and remain unseen," the king of the endermen said, then disappeared in a cloud of purple.

He materialized right next to the zombie king.

"What is this?" Xa-Tul bellowed as he drew his massive broadsword.

Feyd stepped back so that the zombie king could see him better.

"It is I, Feyd," the enderman king said.

"Xa-Tul figured Feyd would show his face again," the monster said. "Are the endermen ready for their assignment?"

"You must first tell us what this is all about," Feyd demanded.

"Feyd is in no position to make requests or ask questions," Xa-Tul replied. "Instructions will be given and the endermen will carry them out. If that is unacceptable, then leave and let Xa-Tul carry out Herobrine's last command alone."

"Fine, Xa-Tul. What are your commands?" Feyd acquiesced.

The king of the zombies glared at Feyd but finally gave him a toothy smile of satisfaction.

"The job of the endermen is to find the User-that-is-not-a-user and keep him away from here," the zombie king said.

"When we find him, will you send your massive army to destroy him? You have more zombies now than you've ever had. There are easily enough monsters to destroy the village of the User-that-is-not-a-user and that idiotic boy-crafter."

"No," snapped Xa-Tul. "That was not the last command of the Maker before leaving Minecraft. Specific instructions were given to Xa-Tul, and the king of the zombies will see them completed.

Destroying some puny villagers was not part of Herobrine's orders."

"Then what were the Maker's commands?" Feyd probed.

Xa-Tul stared at the dark red monster and laughed.

"If the Maker wanted Feyd to know, then the instructions would have been given to the king of the endermen . . . but they were not. Herobrine's last instruction was given to Xa-Tul and only Xa-Tul. Now do as commanded."

How long must I suffer this fool? Feyd thought. *But until I know his plan, I must play along.*

"Very well, we will do as you ask, but—"

"As I *command*," Xa-Tul clarified.

"Right, whatever," Feyd replied. "But when we find him, you will tell me Herobrine's plan, or I will leave Gameknight999 to do whatever he wants to disrupt your preparations."

"Hmm . . ." the zombie king said, thinking. "Agreed."

Feyd nodded his head, then gathered his teleportation powers. The waves of purple mist struggled to coalesce, then formed a solid cloud, allowing him to travel at the speed of thought. He materialized back with his warriors in the shadowy part of the zombie-town.

"Is all well, Sire?" one of the endermen asked.

"For now, yes," Feyd replied. "Our task is to find Gameknight999. This is of the utmost importance. When he is found, you are to report back to me. When we know where the User-that-is-not-a-user is located and what he is doing, then we will have leverage to force the foolish zombie king to tell us his plans."

Feyd's eyes were beginning to glow white with annoyance at his meeting with Xa-Tul.

"Spread the word to all endermen. Find the User-that-is-not-a-user at all costs. Understood?"

The shadowy monsters nodded their heads.

"Then go, and return here when you are successful," Feyd commanded.

The monsters disappeared sporadically as each struggled to form a strong teleportation field. But eventually, they were all gone.

"We will find you, Gameknight999," Feyd said to the darkness that surrounded him. "Then we will exact our revenge on you at last."

He cackled a spine-tingling laugh that echoed through the cavern like the sound of a nightmare, then he disappeared from sight.

CHAPTER 23

BACK TO ZOMBIE-TOWN

Gameknight had sent out riders to the other nearby villages to spread the word about the captive NPCs and Xa-Tul's horde of zombies, in hopes of convincing more warriors to join their group. Many were concerned that the zombie king was amassing a giant army, but when they heard about Herder being taken prisoner, they were all enraged and agreed to help.

Herder was known by every village in Minecraft for his generosity and selflessness: gathering horses for those on the plains, bringing pigs and cows and chickens to those in the desert, and, of course, distributing his wolves throughout every community for protection against the monsters. He had become something of a legend amongst all the villagers. They called him the Animal-whisperer, because he could just speak softly to the animals and they would do his bidding. His willingness to help everyone, coupled with his innocent nature, made the villagers furious when they learned of his capture. This anger galvanized the villages together, making them want to seek revenge. Without this, Gameknight would probably not have been able to convince all the NPCs to come and help.

Gameknight's castle quickly became filled with villagers as they streamed in from all across the Overworld. But as the army grew, so did the demands on the village. Hunters were sent out to bring in food, and farmers harvested all the crops. Groups of warriors were sent to the Nether to collect Nether wart, while large groups were instructed to forage for melons—two necessary ingredients for healing potions. But after a few days of preparation, they were ready.

Using the minecart network, the NPC army moved quickly to Cobbler's village in the savannah. But when they went to the surface of the Overworld, the wolves began to whimper and howl.

"What's wrong with the animals?" Hunter asked, pointing at the pack leader, who was the loudest.

"They miss Herder," Gameknight said. "It's just like Jenny's dog in the physical world; he's named Barky the Physics Dog. He always whines and howls whenever my sister is out of the house. My mom and dad hate it, but with a few snacks, they can get him quiet."

"Sounds like a pretty smart dog," Hunter added with a smile. "He gets what he wants."

"Yep."

Others tried to calm the animals, but there was no sating their grief; they missed Herder terribly.

With the army fully assembled, they now ran across the gray-green landscape with Gameknight out front, the wolf-pack leader, Buck, at his side.

"Come on everyone . . . keep up," the User-that-is-not-a-user said. "Our friends need us."

He shifted to a sprint for a while, then slowed to a run, then walked to give the warriors some rest.

"Creepers to the left!" someone shouted.

"Archers . . . get 'em!" Gameknight yelled.

A group of warriors, led by Hunter, dashed off to the left and fired upon the green monsters. Gameknight wanted to have the element of surprise on his side, and because of that, they had to silence any monster that saw them, or risk word reaching the zombies that the NPCs were coming.

In minutes, the archers returned, Hunter giving him a satisfied smile to show that the threat had been taken care of.

They continued across the savannah in silence. Occasionally, they came across a few more creepers and spiders, but all of them were eliminated by squads of archers before the monsters could escape and report the army's position.

Gameknight could feel the tension in the group building as they went on, but he was lost in his thoughts. The expression on Herder's face as Gameknight ran away into the tunnel tore at his heart. It had been a look of acceptance but also of bravery, like Herder was telling him: *I can handle this.* Herder was so brave, and now Gameknight999 struggled to brush aside feeling like a coward for running away.

But he knew there was no point in dwelling on the past. He refused to see only the bad side of that situation. They'd found this ancient zombie-town and learned that Xa-Tul was amassing a huge army; this information was important, and if they hadn't gone to that zombie-town, then they would still be clueless to the monsters' evil plans. Instead of focusing on what they'd lost that day, Gameknight was focusing on what they had *gained*: knowledge. And glancing around at all the warriors that ran at his side, they had gained more insight than Xa-Tul could have ever imagined.

I'm coming for you, Herder, he thought. *We are coming for* all *of you.*

The words repeated over and over in his head as if it was some kind of magical incantation. He'd made every preparation he could, planned for every possible outcome, but he still knew that nothing was certain. "No battle plan survives first contact with the enemy." That was a popular saying amongst military commanders, and Gameknight had learned its truth all too many times in Minecraft. Still, they would not be dissuaded on this quest.

"Anyone in there?" Hunter asked on his right as she tapped lightly on the Gameknight's helmet.

"Ahh . . . what?" he replied, only half-hearing the question.

"I said, is there anyone in there?" Hunter repeated.

"Yeah, I'm here. I'm just thinking about Herder."

"We all are," she replied. "But if you ask me, we should have—"

"We're here!" Crafter shouted from the front of the group as the sound of the waterfall filled the air.

"Quickly, everyone follow the narrow pass and go through to the cave on the other side," Gameknight said.

He didn't wait for any of them to respond. The User-that-is-not-a-user charged ahead, darting through the falling water with a line of wolves right behind. As he moved into the tunnel, the wolves began acting strange. It was like they were nervous or unsure about what they were doing.

"What's wrong, Buck?" Gameknight said to the alpha male, but the animal just stared up at him and whined. "Don't worry, we'll get Herder back."

When the rest of the army had made it through the falls, they moved carefully forward. The passage dipped downward as it plunged into the flesh of Minecraft. As before, the tunnel twisted this way and that, but this time, torches marked the path from the last time the villagers has visited. Soon, they came to the entrance of the zombie-town. In the distance, they could see the end of the tunnel, a dim green light marking the opening to the objective. With the army twenty blocks or so from the edge of the massive cavern, diggers pulled out pickaxes, and started burrowing into the stone walls.

"Now explain this to me again?" Hunter questioned. "The cave is right there, but we need to make our own tunnels?"

"You remember the passages that led into the zombie-town from all sides?" Gameknight asked.

"Sure," Hunter replied.

"Some of the warriors are going to carve their way to them, then enter from those tunnels, while we go in from the front," Gameknight explained. "The zombies will see our small force here and charge toward us, but then the other warriors will attack their flanks . . . a classic pincer movement. They'll think they have us trapped, but instead, we'll have them surrounded."

"Nice," the redhead replied as she nodded.

Soon, the warriors were through to the other passages. After the forces separated, Gameknight led his squad forward.

The awful smell of the zombies hit him as soon as he moved into the massive cavern, but somehow it didn't seem as bad as last time. Maybe he was getting used to it. Moving about ten blocks into the cavern, Gameknight stopped and banged his sword on his chest plate. The sound echoed off the stone walls, but no moans or growls came in response. The place looked empty.

Suddenly, Buck moved next to Gameknight, sniffed in the air, then let loose a loud sorrowful howl, causing the other wolves to join in. The animal peered up at Gameknight and barked once, then turned and fled back toward the exit and the waterfall, the rest of the wolf pack following close behind.

"Wait!" Gameknight shouted, but it was too late. The wolves had abandoned them.

Before anyone could ask a question, the other warriors stormed out of their tunnels, but no zombies attacked. In fact, the cavern seemed completely empty.

"Where are all the monsters?" Hunter said with a disappointed tone to her voice.

"I don't know," Gameknight replied. "Everyone, move to Digger's tunnel and form up . . . tight formation."

The warriors sprinted to Digger, then formed a tight ball of armor, archers on the outside, swordsmen at the center.

"Move to the next tunnel," Gameknight commanded.

The army moved to the next tunnel, then the next and the next. Each time they found the same thing . . . nothing. Everyone was gone, the zombies and their friends.

"The portal room," Stitcher said.

"Of course," Gameknight exclaimed. "Follow me!"

The User-that-is-not-a-user sprinted across the cratered floor, heading for the stairway that led downward, the walls of the passage glowing with shifting colors. He charged down the steps with both swords in his hands, ready for battle. But like the rest of the cavern, the portal room was empty, only the three glowing obsidian rings standing silently at the far end.

"Where did they all go?" Crafter asked. "It's almost as if Xa-Tul is avoiding a direct confrontation with us. Like he doesn't want to fight."

"But why?" Cobbler replied. "What is that monster afraid of? He outnumbers us ten to one, and he knows the terrain far better than we do. The zombies have every advantage, yet they still run from us."

"Thanks for that inspiring summary," Hunter said.

Stitcher punched her in the arm. The older sister flashed the younger a smile.

"Gameknight!" yelled a voice from the zombie-town.

The User-that-is-not-a-user turned and faced the stairway. He saw an NPC pushing though the crowd. It was Weaver.

"What is it?" Gameknight asked. "Are you OK?"

Weaver nodded his head as he took huge gulps of air.

"I found another portal in one of the side passages," Weaver said.

"Another portal?" Digger said.

"Of course," Crafter said. "There must be two of them. One of the portals leads to the previous zombie-town while the other leads to the next one in the network, just like with our minecart network."

"So how do we know which one the zombies used?" Stitcher queried.

All eyes swiveled to Gameknight999.

"OK, this is your show," Digger said. "What do you want to do?"

The User-that-is-not-a-user glanced up at his friend and saw complete confidence and grim determination in the stocky NPC's blue-green eyes. The portal room was so completely silent; Gameknight thought maybe he'd gone deaf. He turned and scanned the faces of those near him and saw the same expression as Digger's. He could see the confidence they all had in him and his preparations; they were ready for anything.

Gameknight999's heart swelled with pride. This moment, right now, was a great moment in his life, and he knew he must never forget it. All of these people were willing to follow him into certain danger, and none of them had any doubts. He was humbled and felt a tear start to trickle out of his eye.

Reaching up, he wiped it with his sleeve, then turned and faced the shimmering green portal next to him.

"This portal seems just as good as the other. After all, when you don't know where you are going, any direction is the right direction," Hunter said with a laugh. "Let's get this party started. I don't want to miss any of the fun."

The villagers all laughed, many of them slapping Gameknight on the back.

"OK," the User-that-is-not-a-user said in a confident voice. "Then let's bring this party to Xa-Tul."

The NPCs cheered as Gameknight999 stepped into the portal.

CHAPTER 24

ZOMBIE PORTALS

ameknight999 leapt out of the portal and sprinted to one wall. There were zombies in the room. He couldn't see them yet, but he could certainly smell them.

"NPCs in the—" he started to say.

Then a zombie stepped into the portal room, and Gameknight never got the chance to complete his thought. He fell on the creature with his swords in a blur of motion. The monster struggled to defend itself, claws reaching for its attacker, but it quickly disappeared with a *pop*.

"All zombies to the portal chamber!" another creature shouted from the stairway.

Gameknight charged ahead, but now he had Digger on one side and Crafter on the other. The trio sprinted up the steps, only to be confronted by twenty zombies, most clad in golden armor and wielding razor-sharp swords. The monsters saw the three warriors and started to laugh.

"There are only three invaders," one of the zombies growled. "How typically pathetic of the NPCs. This should be easy."

The other zombies laughed.

But then, fifty more warriors charged up out of the portal room and smashed into the creatures. Gameknight slashed at one monster, then rolled to the right and came up swinging at another. He moved so quickly that the monsters didn't know where to look. It was clear to Gameknight that the zombies knew who he was, because they all tried to attack him at the same time. That was foolish. There was enough room for one or two to face him at a time, and that left the other monsters trying to squeeze past their comrades to attack the User-that-is-not-a-user. They never noticed the hundreds of villagers flowing out of the portal room and surrounding them, attacking their flanks, until it was too late.

Monsters growled and moaned as the NPCs moved in from all side. Arrows began to rain down upon them as Hunter and Stitcher climbed the rough-hewn walls and fired their enchanted bows. With deadly arrows falling from above and razor-sharp blades on all sides, the zombies didn't last very long.

Soon, every zombie had been destroyed and the ground was littered with gold armor and balls of XP glowing like tiny little rainbows.

"Collect the armor," Digger commanded. "Squads, check the tunnels to see if they are empty. Archers, get in a defensive formation around this portal room. Swordsmen, get ready to . . ."

Digger moved the warriors with practiced efficiency, placing his pieces on the game board like a chess master. In seconds, the warriors were prepared for a counter-attack, while squads of armored swordsmen checked all of the tunnels that opened into the massive cavern.

For the first time, Gameknight surveyed his surroundings. This zombie-town was like the last one, in that the ground was covered with craters. At the center of the cavern, a tall stone pillar reached up to the high ceiling as if it were the lone support that prevented all the tons of stone and dirt from falling down on them. He knew the rules of physics didn't really work in Minecraft and the ceiling could not fall in on them unless it were made of gravel or sand, but he still felt comforted to see that thick support.

"There's nothing over here," one of the warriors shouted from the opposite side of the cave.

"Or here," said another NPC.

"It seems this one is deserted like the last one," Crafter said.

"Then we keep going," Gameknight growled. "Herder and the other villagers are waiting for us and we can't afford to let them down."

He glanced at the other villagers around him and could still see courage and determination in their eyes.

"Come on, everyone," the User-that-is-not-a-user said.

He ran for the second green portal nestled in a different portal room. The sound of the clanking armor and thundering footsteps behind him reminded the User-that-is-not-a-user that he was not on his own. But the fact was, he didn't care whether the others were following or not; Gameknight999 had friends to save, and nothing was going to stop him. He knew the risks, but instead of focusing on what might happen, Gameknight was focused on how happy he was going to be when Herder was safe again. The image of the lanky boy with the long black hair playing happily with his wolves kept Gameknight's resolve as strong as steel.

He simply refused to give up.

When he reached the stairs that led to the smaller portal chamber, Gameknight charged down without a thought. With his diamond sword in his right hand and his iron blade in his left, he readied himself for battle in case any zombies were hiding down there. Fortunately, the room was empty.

The shimmering green portal stood in the center of a stone chamber, the black obsidian ring lit with a flickering emerald glow. Gameknight moved next to it. He could hear the hum of the portal as the tiny green particles flowed out of the gateway, only to get sucked back in again. But the strange thing was that the humming seemed to stutter and skip, like a scratched CD in his CD player. It was as if the portal itself was having difficulty working—another sign of the mysterious server glitches.

As the warriors gathered around the shimmering gateway, Gameknight turned and stared at them.

"I'm going through," he said. "None of you have to follow me. You can turn around and go home without any shame. I will not stop until I find our friends, and likely one of these portals will lead to a massive army looking to destroy us all. But I am grateful for the help of any who wish to stay with me."

He waited to see if any of the villagers headed up the steps and back toward home. Instead, all of them took a step closer.

"Let's get on with it," Hunter said. "You promised us a party, and that last battle was barely worth noticing."

The warriors laughed.

Gameknight smiled, then turned back to the portal.

"OK, here we go," the User-that-is-not-a-user said.

Gripping both his swords firmly, he sprinted through the portal with the entire army close behind him.

What none of the NPCs noticed before they left was a pair of purple eyes watching from the shadows. Once all the warriors had left the empty zombie-town, the enderman stepped out of the darkness. He gave a chuckle that only the bats heard, but it made the flying creatures squeak with fear.

"The User-that-is-not-a-user is coming . . . perfect," the enderman screeched. "I can't wait to tell Feyd. The king of the endermen will be very pleased with me."

And then the dark creature disappeared in a flickering purple mist.

CHAPTER 25
HEROBRINE'S PLAN

The king of the endermen materialized in a shadowy alcove. It was a huge space, large enough for a couple hundred monsters, as long as they didn't mind standing close together. This probably had been used as some kind of observation platform during the Great Zombie Invasion.

Below him, Feyd saw a massive cavern that stretched out far to the left and right, the walls barely visible in the distance. At the center of the cavern was a circle of eight HP fountains, each one spewing sparkling green embers into the air. They floated down like emerald snowflakes, settling on the zombies that stood nearby and soaking into their skin. The monsters all crowded near the fountains, each one hoping to absorb as much of the life-rejuvenating HP as possible. It was the only way they fed, and it was critical to their survival.

Feyd watched as zombies that were emerging from the portal room pushed through the crowd to get to the HP fountains. Many began to fight amongst themselves as they pushed and shoved to be closer to the precious sparkling green particles.

The number of monsters in the cavern was shocking. Xa-Tul must have gathered a thousand monsters, with more coming out of the portal room every minute. Soon, the number of zombies would rise beyond the capacity of the cave. Feyd was not sure what would happen then.

"This is foolish," the king of the endermen muttered to himself. "With a few carefully-placed explosives, serious damage could be done to that army of decaying creatures. What are you up to, Xa-Tul?"

Just then, another presence began to materialize next to him. Turning, he saw a mist of purple particles trying to form into a cloud, but they sputtered and flickered. Finally, with difficulty, the lavender cloud was sufficient enough to allow the enderman to materialize.

"Sire, I have news," the enderman said quickly. "I have seen him."

"What are you talking about?" Feyd asked.

"I've seen *him* . . . the User-that-is-not-a-user," the monster replied.

"What? Where?"

"He is traveling with a large army of NPCs. They found one of the ancient zombie-towns. After destroying the company of zombies guarding it, they disappeared through one of the portals."

"He will be coming soon . . . goooood," Feyd said, his screechy voice echoing off the stone walls. "Bring all our endermen to this alcove. A momentous event will soon happen . . . the destruction of Gameknight999."

"Yes, my king," the enderman replied before disappearing in a strained cloud of purple mist.

Feyd waited until his warrior was gone, then gathered his teleportation powers about him. Sparkling purple particles began to fill his vision, but they spluttered and gasped as they struggled to create the solid cloud that he needed to make the jump. Finally, the lavender mist was strong enough and he could feel that familiar sensation in the back of his head, as if he were in two places at once . . . then he jumped.

Instantly, he materialized in the portal chamber far below. It was a large room with three dark obsidian rings at one side, the light from the shimmering gateways casting a strange dull glow on the uneven stone walls that shifted from green to purple to pale yellow. Xa-Tul was standing next to the sickly yellow gateway laughing, his bombastic voice filling the portal room. Nearby, two villagers, one older and the other impossibly skinny with long black hair, were digging into the walls of the chamber, slowly widening the entrance so that the nearly-constant flow of monsters from the yellow doorway could exit the portal chamber unabated.

Pushing his way through the tide of decaying green monsters, Feyd moved to the zombie king's side.

"I have news about the User-that-is-not-a-user," the enderman king said.

"What? Gameknight999 . . . tell me, quickly."

"First, you must agree to tell me what your plan is here," Feyd said. "If you do not agree, then I will take my information and go."

"How dare Feyd try to bargain with Xa-Tul!" the zombie yelled.

Feyd peered into the Xa-Tul's eyes, then glanced at all the zombies around him. He was completely surrounded. The king of the endermen gathered his teleportation powers in case he had to flee, but the sparkling purple particles wouldn't answer his command; they flickered around him briefly, then just fizzled out.

"The enderman king has so much confidence that Feyd does not even prepare to teleport away," Xa-Tul said as he reached up to rub his square chin. "Interesting . . . this information must be good. Very well. I agree."

"OK, Gameknight999 has gained access to your portal network," Feyd said.

"How can this be?!" the zombie king bellowed.

"One of my enderman saw him enter the zombie-town where you captured that last bunch of villagers," Feyd explained. "They defeated the pathetic zombies you left there on guard, then went into the green portal. They are likely on their way here . . . now. My servant tells me that he has many NPCs with him. But you have enough zombies to stave off any threat he can offer. You might lose some zombies, but you will surely destroy that army of rabble that follows him."

"No . . . a battle is not what Xa-Tul wants," the zombie king said.

"Then what *is* it that you want?" Feyd asked. "What is your plan?"

The big zombie shoved some monsters aside so that he could pace back and forth across the portal room.

"I was given one last command by the Maker, Herobrine, right before he disappeared through the gateway of light," the zombie king said. He stopped pacing and turned to glare at Feyd. "His voice echoed in my mind when he told me that I would be the instrument of the ultimate revenge against all the

NPCs. He gave me one single command and told me that it was the most important thing I would ever do."

The zombie king stepped up close to the endermen so that he could hear him over the din of growling monsters that flowed out of the portal.

"What did he tell you to do?" Feyd probed eagerly.

"He told me to bring all the zombies to this server," Xa-Tul said.

"Why . . . are we going to attack?"

"No," the zombie king answered. "He told me that bringing every zombie here to this world would destabilize the pyramid of servers. Herobrine told me this would cause the pyramid to collapse, crashing all the servers."

"What?"

"We will destroy all the villagers in one single stroke," Xa-Tul said, his voice growing louder, filled with excitement and joy. "At the moment of their destruction, the villagers and Gameknight999 will know that this is Herobrine's last act. They will rue the day that they ever rose up against him. It will be the Maker's last great revenge."

"You fool! Your plan will destroy all the monsters as well!" Feyd screeched.

Xa-Tul growled and placed his large clawed hand on the hilt of his golden broadsword.

"Feyd dares to talk back to the king of the zombies like that?" Xa-Tul growled.

"Don't you understand? If you cause the servers to crash, then *every* living thing on the servers will also be destroyed."

The big zombie stared back at Feyd with a look of confusion on his face.

"That means us!" Feyd screamed. "The monsters will be destroyed with the villagers. We will all die."

"No!" Xa-Tul snapped. "The Maker would never do that. Herobrine would never destroy the monsters; they are his loyal servants."

"Herobrine only cared about Herobrine, and that led to his final destruction," the enderman king said. "Now he wants to kill the villagers, even if it means the destruction of the monsters as well."

"Xa-Tul does not believe Feyd. The Maker has a plan to save the monsters when the destruction happens. Xa-Tul has faith in the Maker to save us."

"The Maker is dead!" Feyd yelled. "I will not allow this madness to happen."

This time, the zombie king drew his sword.

"The king of the endermen must not interfere with Herobrine's revenge. Leave this place now, while you still have your life."

Without waiting for an answer, the zombie swung his sword at the enderman. This time, with the enderman's full concentration, Feyd was able to gather enough teleportation particles to jump back to the raised alcove.

"The fool. He will destroy us all," Feyd said.

He glared down at the zombies with vile contempt.

"The zombies are like idiotic sheep. They will follow any command without giving it the least bit of thought. We must somehow control the situation and keep Xa-Tul from killing all of us."

And then an idea came to him. It was a dangerous idea, but these were dangerous times, and right now, he had no choice. With his eyes glowing bright white, Feyd teleported from the chamber and began to put his plan into motion.

CHAPTER 26
ESCAPE

Herder slowly moved along the wall, digging into the stone and dirt wall as he went.

"Bookman, this way," the skinny NPC said in a low voice.

The village's librarian, Bookman, glanced up at the lanky youth and nodded, then slowly walked toward him, carving into the stone with every step. It was slow to move like this through the chamber, but the zombies didn't seem to care where they went, as long as they were digging.

Carefully, the duo dug their way along the jagged walls until they were out of the portal room and in the main chamber.

"Did you hear what the zombie king said?" Herder whispered.

Bookman nodded his boxy head.

"If he is able to crash the pyramid of servers, it will destroy everything," Bookman said. "I once read something called *The Virus* in one of the libraries in a stronghold. It was a story speculating about how Herobrine came into the server, and how none of the villagers or monsters or anything were alive before his entrance." He paused to push his gray hair out of his face, then wiped his brow on his white sleeve, now tattered and stained with dirt and sweat. "If they crash the servers, who knows what will happen? Likely we will all die, and without Herobrine and his virus in the system, we will not respawn."

"You mean . . . " Herder said, but couldn't finish the sentence as his mind filled with dread. Bookman nodded.

"Yes, everyone and everything will go back to just being computer code. Our bodies might respawn, maybe, but there will be no mind within our heads, no thoughts, no ideas . . . nothing. Essentially, we will all be . . . "

"Dead," Herder breathed.

"Exactly."

"We must warn the others," Herder said, a scowl creasing his unibrow.

"You mean the other prisoners?" Bookman asked.

"No, Gameknight999," Herder said. "He will know what to do."

"What are you . . ." Bookman started to say, then quickly stopped. "Shhhh . . ."

Quickly, both villagers went back to digging as one of the meaner zombie guards walked nearby to check on their progress. They had learned that this one was called Ma-Kul and was especially vicious. The zombie didn't mind raking an NPC's back with his razor-sharp claws if he didn't think they were working hard enough.

"What are these two pathetic villagers talking about?" Ma-Kul growled.

The two villagers remained silent and continued digging. Herder and the other NPCs had learned that if they answered, then it meant they weren't digging, which meant instant punishment from the guards.

"Keep digging, or else," the zombie guard growled, then walked toward one of the HP fountains. Herder realized he had been holding his breath and finally exhaled as the monster passed.

"Follow me," the skinny boy said.

With their pickaxes ringing against the stone walls, the pair of villagers moved to a dark corner of the cavern. They knew there was a deep tunnel there, but the diggers had eventually hit lava and abandoned digging in that direction.

"Come on, we need to dig," Herder said.

"But there is lava all around here. If we break a stone block that is next to a lava lake, the molten stone might flow onto us."

"Then we'll have to be careful," Herder replied. "Besides, the zombies won't be looking for us over here then. We must get out of here and warn Gameknight999 of the zombie plan."

He moved to one wall that was lined with dirt. "Let's start here."

Reaching into his inventory, he drew his enchanted shovel that he'd been keeping hidden. It had the *Efficiency II* enchantment on it—a gift from Crafter. Herder tore into the brown cubes, making them disappear with just a touch of his shovel. He dug straight into the wall, not even bothering to make a hole two blocks high, but instead just tore into the blocks that were at face height. The iron shovel drilled a hole four blocks deep without hitting any lava. He then dug the blocks out at his feet so that the hole was now two high by four deep.

Moving to the end of the mini-tunnel, he repeated the process. But after digging up two more blocks of dirt, he hit lava. The orange liquid lit the tunnel with a warm light. Quickly, he pulled out a block of cobblestone and plugged the leak.

Turning to the right, he dug in a new direction. After going a dozen blocks, he hit lava again. After each collision with the deadly melted rock, he changed direction and continued to tunnel, creating a random, zigzag path through the stone and dirt.

"We aren't getting anywhere," Bookman whispered, his voice echoing off the walls of the dark tunnel. "And I can't see anything."

The old NPC pulled out a torch and was about to place it on the ground, when they heard a scratching sound, like claws gouging into the stone ground.

"Quick, put out the torch," Herder whispered. Bookman put away the torch, plunging them into darkness again.

"This zombie saw something in this tunnel. It was some kind of light," they heard a zombie say.

Herder could hear the razor-sharp claws clicking on the stone floor as guards moved through the circuitous passage.

"Co-Zir is crazy," said another zombie.

"Something was there," Co-Zir growled. "If something is found, Co-Zir will be promoted and will no longer be a 'C.'"

"Crazy zombies are not promoted," the other zombie laughed.

"Er-Tom will not be laughing when Co-Zir is promoted to an 'F.' Perhaps this zombie will be named Fa-Zir with this discovery," Co-Zir said.

They were getting closer. Herder could now hear their animalistic breathing. The stench of their rotting bodies was beginning to fill the passage.

"Get back," Herder whispered, pushing Bookman against the wall. Quickly, he pulled out two blocks of cobblestone and sealed the tunnel, separating them from the zombies. "Hopefully, they will think there is lava beyond those blocks and just go away."

Bookman did not answer; he was terrified beyond the ability to speak. If they were found back in these tunnels, they would surely be killed, and both of the villagers knew it. Just then, a fist pounded on the cobblestone block. It shook with the strength of the blow, causing dust to fall from the walls and ceiling. Herder started to shake, then accidently dropped his pick. It clattered to the ground, the iron tool ringing like a struck bell.

"What was that?" Co-Zir growled.

"That was nothing. Just an echo," Er-Tom replied.

"No, this zombie heard something," the first zombie insisted.

"Co-Zir is welcome to stay, but this zombie is going to continue the patrol. If the expansion to the other side of the cavern is not complete, Ma-Kul will punish us."

Herder could hear the zombie walk away, his heavy footsteps fading way.

"Come!" shouted the monster.

"Co-Zir knows there was a sound," the zombie muttered to the stone, then turned and walked away, his scratchy, pounding footsteps slowly fading away.

Herder waited for at least five minutes before daring to remove the cobblestone. But when they opened their tiny cell, they found the tunnel again empty.

"That was close," Bookman said.

Herder nodded.

"We need to hurry," the lanky boy said.

Swinging his pick at the stone wall, he started to dig again, moving to the left and right as he continued to skirt the edges of the underground lava lake.

Stepping up to a new wall, Herder dug up four blocks of stone at head height. Then the last block shattered, and light streamed into the narrow passage. They both jumped back, thinking the light was from deadly lava, but when the hole did not fill with molten stone, they moved forward again. Both villagers stared into the hole. A torch was visible in the distance, illuminating what looked like a thick wooden column.

"What is that?" Bookman asked.

Herder looked at his friend and smiled.

"It's an abandoned mineshaft," Herder said, his voice bubbling with excitement.

"That means the minecart network will be nearby somewhere," Bookman added.

Herder nodded his boxy head again, causing his long black hair to fall across his dirty face. Suddenly, the sound of more clawed feet echoed off the passage walls.

"They're coming! Hurry!" Bookman said.

Herder tore into the stone, opening a passage to the abandoned mineshaft. The sound of zombie feet was getting louder.

"Hurry," he pleaded.

When they reached the empty shaft, Herder could see minecart rails stretching out into the distance. Wooden beams held up the walls and ceiling, and torches were placed here and there to provide just enough light to see.

"Quickly, we have to go," Bookman said.

"No, they will only follow," Herder replied.

"What are you talking about?"

"Here, take this," the young boy said, handing over his enchanted shovel. "Find the User-that-is-not-a-user and tell him what is happening here. He will know what to do. Warn the other villagers and have them prepare. We will need all the warriors we can find. Tell Gameknight to remember Crafter's Great Uncle Weaver and 'follow-the-leader.' He will know what I mean."

"But you can't—"

Before the old man could finish his sentence, Herder shoved him backward into the abandoned mine, then sealed the tunnel with cobblestone. Reaching into his inventory, he pulled out an extra pick and a stone shovel and dropped them on the ground. He then pulled out his pickaxe and started to dig, just as Ma-Kul turned the corner.

"What is this idiotic villager doing here?" the monster demanded.

Herder could see Co-Zir standing behind the larger zombie, smiling a toothy grin.

"I'm . . . ahh . . . finding the edges of the lava lake," Herder said, trying to sound confident; he did a poor job.

"The villager lies," Ma-Kul said.

The violent zombie slapped Herder across the face, hard. It knocked the lanky boy to the ground, causing his head to spin as his vision blurred for just an instant. Pain echoed through his skull.

"Where is the other villager . . . the gray-haired one?" the zombie asked.

Herder pointed to the pick and shovel that floated on the ground.

"The lava got him," Herder lied.

The zombie glared at the items, then grunted as if upset at the loss, not because he was sad, but because it was one less worker who would help expand the cave.

"Get up, idiot, and pick up those items. They are still useful," Ma-Kul said.

He then turned to the smaller zombie.

"Good work finding these villagers," the commander said. "Co-Zir will be promoted to En-Zir. Keep watch on them; they cannot be trusted."

The newly-promoted zombie nodded his head.

"Take this skinny fool back with the others," Ma-Kul ordered. "Villagers cannot be left alone. And punish this one for letting the gray-haired NPC fall into the lava. They are fools. They are all fools."

En-Zir reached down and grabbed Herder's arm, his claws digging into the young boy's arm. He yanked him to his feet and shoved him next to the items on the ground. Herder bent over and picked up the shovel and pick, then turned and walked out of the tunnel. The two zombies followed right behind Herder, kicking him with their clawed feet if he moved too slowly. In the darkness, though, neither of the monsters saw the satisfied grin on the lanky boy's face.

Hurry, Gameknight999, hurry, Herder thought. *We need you now more than ever.*

CHAPTER 27

EMPTY TOWNS

Gameknight leapt out of the portal and into the small stone room. He scanned the room for monsters, his gaze penetrating into every shadow. There were none. He moved to the foot of the stairs and waited for the other villagers. In seconds, the portal room in the zombie-town was filled with warriors.

Hunter and Stitcher moved to his side as more NPCs poured out from the sparkling green portal.

"Come on," the User-that-is-not-a-user said.

Without waiting for a reply, he charged up the steps and into the zombie-town, his dual swords ready for slashing claws and snarling teeth. But like the last one and the one before that, the zombie-town was empty. The only creatures stirring in the massive cavern were the occasional bats that flittered about in the shadows, their high-pitched squeaks echoing off the rocky walls.

"Another empty zombie-town. What's going on?" Gameknight grumbled. "Where have all the zombies gone?"

"Maybe they heard you were coming and they're scared?" Hunter joked.

Gameknight flashed her an angry glare, then turned and moved into one of the tunnels that pierced the side of the cavern, a group of soldiers following. Crafter and Digger took a second group of warriors to another passage.

Standing before the dark opening, the User-that-is-not-a-user could hear only the echo of bats and the dripping of water. Nothing moaned or growled or shuffled clumsily across the stone floor. The passage was completely empty. Glancing at Crafter, he saw the same confusion on his face. The zombies were gone.

The army spread out across the cavern into all of the tunnels and alcoves, searching for any evidence that the creatures had ever been here. But it was as if the cavern had been scrubbed clean.

"There's nothing here!" Digger shouted in frustration, his voice filling the silence like a clap of thunder.

"Everyone to the next portal!" Gameknight shouted.

He sprinted to the smaller portal chamber, which held just a single green portal. This lone gateway would lead to the next underground chamber on the zombie network. The rest of the army converged to the same point, their armored feet pounding across the uneven floor and filling the cavern with thunder. They gathered around the entrance to the small room and waited for instructions.

"What's the plan?" Stitcher asked.

"We keep searching!" Gameknight snapped. "We must find them."

"You're right, but so far, all we've found are empty zombie-towns," Crafter said as he approached his friend. "We can't just keep blundering blindly from village to village."

Gameknight sighed. Maybe Cobbler was right.

The image of Herder being grabbed by decaying green hands burst into his mind; the terrified expression on Herder's face was etched deep into his soul. Hunter moved next to him and placed a reassuring hand on his arm.

"Don't worry. We'll find him," she said in a soft voice.

"He was my responsibility," Gameknight growled. "He's been my responsibility ever since he joined the fight against the monsters of Minecraft."

"I know," she replied.

"I was supposed to watch out for him and keep him safe," he said. "But look what I've done. He's captured. Who knows what they are doing to him? What if . . ."

"NO!" Hunter snapped. "There are no *what-if*'s, there is only what you are going to do about it right now. If you go down the *what-if* path, then you will just give power to your anxiety and fear. Instead, we are going to do something to help him. You got that?"

He mumbled something unintelligible as he lowered his eyes to the ground. Hunter smacked him in the head with her bow. Gameknight's diamond helmet rang like a bell for a moment as anger grew from within. He glared at her.

"That's better," Hunter said. "You need to get mad about all this and then figure out how to solve our problem. But giving up or panicking or blaming yourself will help no one, least of all, Herder."

Gameknight growled, but this time it was not directed at Hunter, but at the zombies and Xa-Tul.

That monster had taken his friend and he was going to get him back.

"Now, what are we going to do?" Hunter asked. "Answer quick or I'll smack you in the head again."

The User-that-is-not-a-user glanced at his friend and scowled, then turned and faced the rest of the army.

"We're going to the next village. If it's empty, then we return to Crafter's village and examine some old maps. I figure they are in one of the ancient zombie-towns from the Great Zombie Invasion. Maybe they aren't even on this portal network."

"Now we're talking!" Hunter said.

"Come on, everyone," Crafter said. "Let's get to the next town, fast!"

The villagers cheered, then ran down the steps and charged into the green portal that would take them to the next portal. The last one to take the stairs down to the small stone room was Cobbler. He had a downcast appearance and a permanently depressed expression on his square face.

"What's wrong Cobbler?" Gameknight asked.

"I think maybe I should just go back to the village," the young boy said. "I think I'll just bring bad luck with me."

The User-that-is-not-a-user could understand how the NPC felt; he felt the same, but he couldn't let Cobbler feel bad. It was in his nature to help where he could.

"Cobbler, Crafter has talked to you about this, and Stitcher, too. Now you're going to hear it from me. You need to understand that good luck and bad luck are all the same," Gameknight explained. "It just depends on how you interpret it. If you focus on the doom and gloom, that's what you will find surrounding you. But if you search for the good in things around you, the positive will come through."

"Really?" Cobbler mumbled. "What's good about being here, right now?"

Gameknight glanced around at the empty zombie-town. He could hear the last of the villagers going through the portal and figured they were alone. But then Hunter, Stitcher, Digger, and Crafter came slowly up the steps and stood behind their friend. And then he knew exactly what to say.

"Let me ask you this, Cobbler. Did you ever think you would see the inside of a zombie-town?"

"Of course not," the boy answered.

"Look how beautiful all the HP fountains are. They're like a constant flow of fireworks coming out of the ground."

Cobbler stared at the fountains and shrugged.

"See all the different colors in the floor and walls? They used every kind of block you could imagine to build their town. It's like a parade of color out here."

The young boy turned around and surveyed the village, this time a little longer than the fountain. He then faced Gameknight and shrugged again. Now, Hunter and Stitcher stepped forward and stood behind Cobbler. Gameknight smiled as he peered at the faces of his friends.

"And look around you," the User-that-is-not-a-user continued. "You are surrounded by friends who will help you with anything you need. Stitcher can see the good in anything. Hunter can make you realize that you are braver than you ever realized. Digger can teach you what it means to be a leader and take care of others. And Crafter . . . well, Crafter can be the greatest friend you ever thought possible. And when you are with these NPCs, no matter what the circumstances are, you are always surrounded by good."

He paused and took a step forward, then peered into the young boy's eyes.

"If you search for the good, you will find it," Gameknight999 said. "I just learned that a few minutes ago when Hunter smacked me in the head, and I will never let you forget it, because you are part of Crafter's village now. That means you are family, so get used to it."

Cobbler gazed up at him, and a tiny square tear tumbled down his cheek.

"Really?" he asked.

Gameknight nodded his head, and then, for the first time, Gameknight saw Cobbler smile. It was the kind that stretched from ear to ear and lit up his eyes.

"Now come on," Gameknight said. "Let's find our friends."

CHAPTER 28

THE VEIL IS LIFTED

Gameknight was doing his best to stay positive and remain a good role model for Cobbler, but his frustration grew with every empty zombie-town they found. The army went through cave after cave, finding the same thing: nothing. No monsters or evidence of their enslaved friends were found. It was as if these zombie-towns had never housed a single monster ever before. But the User-that-is-not-a-user knew better. The one thing the monsters could not eliminate was the smell of decaying flesh. Every one of the abandoned caves still had a faint odor that made everyone's stomach turn just a bit.

Finally, after the fourth zombie-town, Gameknight conceded.

"Let's go back to Crafter's village," the User-that-is-not-a-user said. "This is getting us nowhere."

The other villagers agreed, and followed their trail back to the first zombie-town. They reached the hidden entrance behind the waterfall in a few hours, then ran most of the way back to the nearby village. When they reached the crafting chamber, the NPCs used the minecart network to get back to Crafter's village.

Once they were home, Crafter went to the library with Digger, pouring over old maps and books about the Great Zombie Invasion. Of course, the real knowledge lay in the libraries of the strongholds. But they were too far away to be of any use. Besides, the last time they had ventured to the stronghold, Gameknight999 and his friends had had to face the Swarm, a massive group of deadly silverfish. None of them really wanted to do that again, unless absolutely necessary. And by the time they reached one of those hidden underground structures, Xa-Tul would have likely completed his task, whatever that was, and their friends would be dead—or worse. No, they had to solve this problem here . . . and now.

Clustering around the village's well, the NPCs debated what to do: ride out on horseback and search for them, go back to the zombie-towns, go to the stronghold . . . every idea was discussed until arguments ensued, but Gameknight stayed clear of the debates. He knew the solution did not lie in a book or out on the plains or in the empty zombie-towns; it would be found somewhere else.

Instead, he stood at the village's gates and gazed out across the grasslands that surrounded the village. The newly-planted forest that lay just beyond them had shown a bit of growth, and the trees that had been treated to a healthy dose of bone meal stood tall, drinking in the waning light from the setting sun.

Pacing back and forth, Gameknight tried to imagine the solution to this problem, hoping the pieces of the puzzle would fall into place, but nothing materialized through the fog of uncertainty that clouded his mind. He had no idea how to save Herder and the other NPCs, and this uncertainty threatened to fill him with another emotion: fear.

Just then, a commotion broke out within the village. A voice rose up out of the collection of wooden buildings, yelling as loudly as possible.

"Come quick!" someone shouted. "Everyone come to the watchtower!"

Gameknight sprinted for the tower, his nerves stretched to their limits. When he reached the tall cobblestone structure, he saw it surrounded by the villagers. Pushing his way through, he wormed his way to the center of the crowd. Seated on the ground was an NPC who appeared completely exhausted. He was leaning against the side of the watchtower, his head tipped to one side. Crafter knelt at his side, quietly speaking to him. The exhausted villager wore a dirty white smock with a tattered gray stripe running down the middle, his hair matching the stripe's color. His face was pale and his breathing strained. Gameknight could tell he was near death.

"Bookman, what happened?" Crafter asked.

It's Bookman! The thought burst into Gameknight's head like one of Crafter's fireworks. He was one of the villagers who had been captured with Herder. The User-that-is-not-a-user peered down at the NPC to see if he had any zombie wounds. His arms were scratched as if cut by a thousand knives. The palms of his hands were almost raw, with blisters and cuts from probably some kind of terrible torture. But most of all, the villager was completely exhausted, his HP dangerously low. It was possible that he would not survive.

Someone handed the aged NPC a piece of steak. He eagerly devoured the meat, which helped his hunger a little, but his HP was still nearly gone; food might not be enough to save him. A piece of melon was handed to Bookman, who took it and tore into it as if it were his last meal.

If only we had a Notch apple, Gameknight thought.

"Get out of the way," said a scratchy voice from the back of the crowd. "Give me room or I'll hit you with a potion of blindness and just push you out of the way. Now MOVE!"

The villagers quickly parted, letting an old woman with a purple smock step through, the green stripe on the front of her smock decorated with multiple stains and spills. It was Morgana, the village's witch. As she neared, Morgana pulled out a splash potion of healing and threw it onto the exhausted NPC. The bottle instantly shattered, throwing liquid across Bookman's body. Bright red sparkles floated over him for just an instant, but then he sat up a little straighter. His pale skin began to fill with a rosy hue as his breathing eased and became more regular. Looking up at the villagers that surrounded him, a smile slowly spread across his wrinkled face. He reached out and gladly accepted a loaf of bread from another villager.

"Where's the User-that-is-not-a-user?" the old NPC said between bites.

"Here," Gameknight said as he moved forward and stared down at him. "What happened? Where is everyone? Is Herder still . . ."

He couldn't finish the question.

"Yes, Herder is alive and well," Bookman answered between bites.

A wave of relief washed over Gameknight like a cleansing tidal wave. His neck muscles relaxed and the knots in his back suddenly disappeared. He hadn't realized how tense he'd been until that moment. He felt like he could finally breathe again.

A solemn expression came across Bookman's face. "At least he was when he helped me escape," the old NPC said. "Herder sacrificed himself so that I could get away. He stayed behind, and drew the zombies off my trail. Without his bravery, I'm sure the zombies would have caught me."

Gameknight's heart skipped a beat. "Do you think he's . . ."

Bookman shrugged, not letting the User-that-is-not-a-user finish the question. "I don't know."

"Tell us, do you know where they are?" Crafter asked.

Bookman nodded his square head as he finished the bread, then started on a huge red apple.

"Are there a lot of zombies with them?" Hunter said as she pushed through the crowd.

The old NPC stopped eating and looked up at the redhead, then glanced at Gameknight999, terror showing in his eyes.

"What is it?" Crafter demanded.

He kept his gaze fixed on the User-that-is-not-a-user, then spoke, his voice cracking fear.

"There are hundreds of zombies there," Bookman said. "No, not hundreds . . . thousands and thousands. More than you could ever count. They're everywhere, crowded into a single zombie-town, with more coming every minute."

"What are they doing?" Gameknight questioned. "Are they getting ready for war?"

The old librarian shook his head, the color in his face now fading a bit. Gameknight could see the villager's eyes filling with dread.

"No . . . worse," Bookman replied. "The zombie king is bringing *all* the zombies from *all* the servers here, to this one."

"Why would he do . . ." Gameknight started, but Bookman held up a hand and stopped him.

"Herobrine ordered Xa-Tul to crash the server. The zombie king believes it will destroy all of the NPCs on this server; it is Herobrine's last revenge on us for standing up to him."

"But that won't just crash *this* server, it will . . ." Crafter stopped talking as an expression of horror covered his boxy face.

Bookman nodded.

"What?" Hunter said. "What are you not saying?"

"If Xa-Tul does this, it will destabilize everything," Crafter said.

"So?" Hunter replied.

"So it could destroy the pyramid of server planes, destroying them all. He could crash the entire Minecraft universe."

"But the servers would restart, right?" Digger asked.

"Maybe," Gameknight answered. "But will all of you still be alive? When I run my own server, the villagers aren't alive. They are just—sorry, no offense—just mindless things wandering around without a purpose or a thought or a mind. Something brought all the Minecraft creatures on the pyramid of servers to life long ago. Will that happen again, or will all of you just die and cease to exist?"

"I'd rather not find out the answer to that question," Hunter said, a scowl creasing her unibrow.

"He must be stopped," Crafter growled.

"But how?" Stitcher asked. "Bookman said they had thousands of zombies."

"We'll need more villagers, but we don't have time to send the word out," Gameknight said.

"Herder took care of that," Bookman said as he slowly climbed to his feet. "After he helped me to escape, Herder told me to warn all the villagers as I came through the minecart network. I went through at least ten villages on the way here and told them what was happening. They are sending riders out in all directions and gathering everyone they can find." He turned and stared straight into Gameknight's eyes. "Herder said you would know what to do with all these warriors. He was confident that you would come and save them all."

"That will give us a couple hundred warriors, but that's not enough to face thousands of zombies," Hunter pointed out.

"Herder said one more thing that I didn't understand, but he said you would," Bookman continued. "He said something about Crafter's Great Uncle Weaver and 'follow-the-leader.' Does that make sense to you?"

Suddenly, the puzzle pieces began to tumble around in Gameknight's head. "Of course . . . like on my server . . . TNT-Run," the User-that-is-not-a-user mumbled to himself.

"What are you talking about?" Hunter asked.

"You'll see," Gameknight replied. "Are the TNT blocks ready?"

"Sure," Morgana answered, her scratchy voice sounding like sandpaper on rough wood. "You brought back a lot of gunpowder from the creeper hive, but I only used what was needed for all those splash potions. We've been making explosives with what's left."

"Excellent. We're going to need it all," Gameknight said with a smile.

"What do you have in mind?" Hunter inquired.

"Something incredibly dangerous and reckless and probably idiotic," Gameknight said. "We're going to teach the zombies how to play TNT-Run, but unfortunately for them, they'll be the recipients of the explosives."

"Perfect," she replied, a wide grin growing across her square face. "We'll treat the monsters to a little game of Zombie-Run."

Gameknight smiled at her as he nodded his head.

"We don't have much time, so I'll need everyone's help," the User-that-is-not-a-user explained. "Here's what I need people to do . . ."

And as Gameknight explained the plan, he realized how incredible risky this plan would be. And if they failed, it would mean the destruction of everything. Icicles of fear stabbed into him, but he knew they had no choice.

Don't worry, Herder, Gameknight thought. *I'm coming for you . . . we all are.*

CHAPTER 29

THE GATHERING STORM

The iron-clad NPCs all piled into minecarts, one after another, each person placing their tiny metal car down on the rails right behind the person in front of them. They shot through the underground tunnels like a river of unstoppable flowing metal, Gameknight at the head. His rage toward what Xa-Tul was planning was like rocket fuel, driving the NPCs' resolve and fanning the flames of their anger.

The sound of hundreds of wheels clattering against the metal rails filled the passageway with the sound of a million castanets. To the User-that-is-not-a-user, it was reassuring. He knew all these warriors would do whatever was necessary to stop the zombie king and find the NPC prisoners. Their confidence in him and his plan made Gameknight feel proud, yet at the same time, worried. But before he could give those echoing voices of dread any attention, his minecart burst into a brightly-lit crafting chamber.

He stepped out and looked around. The chamber was filled with an entire community of villagers, each one armed to the teeth. Every NPC held a metal cart and was ready to add their strength to the growing army. Gameknight999 glanced at the villagers in the chamber, his heart filling with pride. They were all there, just like those behind him, because they had faith in him. He was proud and honored but also terrified—more lives to protect.

Sighing, the User-that-is-not-a-user placed his cart on the next track and pushed off. When the cart rolled across the red-glowing powered rails, it shot forward and plunged into the next tunnel, a long snake of iron boxes following behind.

With each crafting chamber they traversed, another fifty to seventy villagers joined the cavalcade. Gameknight could sense the excitement in the warriors. They were anxious to free their friends and stop the zombies. But as they moved closer and closer to their destination, the excitement slowly changed to apprehension and dread. After three more villages, everyone stopped talking and just focused straight ahead, staring at the armored person in front of them. They all knew what danger lay in store for them. There would be thousands of monsters eager to take every last bit of their HP. But the villagers had Gameknight999 and his crazy plan on their side.

Just then, laughter exploded somewhere behind him, and shouts of "Zombie-Run!" percolated up the line of minecarts. Hunter must have told the new NPCs about Gameknight's plan. The chuckles and snickers were a welcome relief to the growing tension. As they moved through more villages, the jokes and laughter grew and tension slowly turned to determination.

Gameknight saw the end of the tunnel brightening; they were almost to the last crafting chamber. When he emerged into the brightly-lit cave, he jumped out of his cart and placed it on the new track. As he pushed off, he noticed the new additions to the army were watching him with optimistic eyes. They were all putting their lives in his hands and hoping to come out of this thing alive.

Gameknight remembered something his mother, a person who saw the good in everything, had once told him. "Good comes in many flavors," she had said. "Sometimes it's the difference between spilling half your drink and spilling all your drink. Spilling half seems bad, but it's better than losing everything. Finding the good in a thing is about perspective and how you look at the world around you. There is good in everything, if you want to find it. The hard part is *wanting* to find it." These words resonated within Gameknight's mind. He refused to focus on the fact that some of the NPCs might never return home. Instead, he thought about stopping Xa-Tul and saving the countless villagers across *all* the server planes. And with this thought, the fearful thoughts seemed to drift away a little.

Finally, they reached the last crafting chamber. But this time, the chamber was empty.

"Hello?" Gameknight yelled. "Where is everyone?"

His voice echoed off the walls of the empty chamber. More warriors rolled into the huge cavern behind him, many of them putting their minecarts on the chests nearby, others just dropping them on the ground. Suddenly, Bookman was at his side, his wild gray hair sticking out from under his iron helmet.

"They're probably on the surface," the old NPC explained. "I figured it was impossible to find that old abandoned mine again, so I told their crafter to find the entrance to the zombie-town. We can . . ."

His words were lost as more minecarts came rattling into the chamber. Gameknight stared at Bookman, then pointed to his ears, gesturing that he couldn't hear anything he was saying. The old villager nodded his head, then sprinted up the steps that led out of the crafting chamber, the User-that-is-not-a-user fast on his heels.

After traversing the tunnels and climbing the long vertical ladder, Gameknight and Bookman finally made it to the watchtower. But to his surprise, they still found no one; the tower was completely deserted.

The User-that-is-not-a-user flashed Bookman a concerned look, then peered at Crafter as he emerged from the vertical shaft. The young NPC surveyed the watchtower. When he noticed it empty, his unibrow raised in concern.

"Let's get outside and see where everyone is hiding," Hunter said as she stepped into the room.

Gameknight flashed her a glance, then stepped up to the door. Nervously, he grasped the doorknob and gave it a turn. The wooden door squeaked as it slowly swung open.

"Let's get moving," Hunter snarled, and shoved Gameknight through the doorway.

He was about to turn around and glare at her when the village square erupted in boisterous cheers. There were hundreds of NPCs clustered around the village's well. They were clad in armor of every kind: iron, leather, diamond, and gold. Some wore mismatched pieces, while a few had no armor at all. They waved their weapons and banged their weapons against armor or stone as he approached. Gameknight was overwhelmed with the welcome and moved to tears.

Running to the well, he jumped up on the narrow stone wall and turned to face the warriors. He held his hands up over his head to quiet the crowd as the rest of the army flowed out of the cobblestone watchtower.

"Where is your crafter?" Gameknight asked once everyone was out of the crafting tunnel and crowded within the bulging village.

An NPC dressed in a black smock, a gray striping running down the center, stepped forward.

"Did you find the entrance to the zombie-town?" the User-that-is-not-a-user asked. The crafter nodded his boxy head.

"Bookman gave us an idea about where to search. We went where he told us and found a tunnel that led deep underground in a forest biome nearby. It led to a place where a large underground lake met a river of lava. The moans of all those zombies can be heard right through the stone walls. We have warriors there right now . . . come."

Gameknight glanced at Hunter and Stitcher, who stood nearby. He was a little nervous, but their smiles buoyed his spirits. Leaping off the wall, the User-that-is-not-a-user walked to the village gates and gazed out across the lush grasslands to the forest that lay in the distance. Behind him, he could hear the clatter of armored villagers as everyone walked through the village. A handful of warriors ran forward with this village's crafter. As the army flowed out of the village gates, Gameknight stepped aside and just watched.

Hunter moved to his side and lightly punched him in the arm.

"Who would have thought we'd ever see an army this big again?" she said, then lowered her voice. "I was kinda hoping this would never happen again . . . you know, a massive war. We had the one at the Source, and then the one on the Ocean Shore, and then that one in the Nether with Herobrine, and now this one. I'm kinda getting tired of fighting."

"I never thought I'd hear that coming from you," Gameknight said.

"You know, I don't *like* to fight . . . I'm just really good at it," she said with a smile, then became very serious. "Every time I'm in a battle, I think about my village and when it was wiped out by the vile ghast, Malacoda. It just makes me lose control, but I want that time to be over. I don't want to think about what has been lost anymore. I just want to think about what great things will come next."

"Those are wise words," Crafter said as he approached, Digger walking right behind.

"Who would have ever thought wisdom would be coming from me?" Hunter said with a laugh.

But no one else laughed.

"None of us are surprised," Digger said in a deep voice.

Gameknight and Crafter nodded their heads.

"Whatever. Let's get going before we miss all the fun," the redhead said as she pulled out her bow and merged into the river of armored villagers that were heading off toward the forest.

Gameknight peered at Crafter and shrugged, then ran after her.

The army ran across the grassy rolling hills without anyone taking a break. Armor clinked and clanked as they jogged, making a sound that reminded Gameknight of a junkyard wind chime. The noise trickled across out from the head of the column and the rear, surrounding him in sound. It was comforting to know that so many people were around him. Gameknight wished they had horses for the troops but knew they could never have collected enough in time. Regardless, the NPCs were determined to see this through, and no one complained about running across the biome.

Quickly, they reached the forest that sat against the plains. Oaks and birches stood tall in the waning light of the afternoon. Long shadows began to creep out from the base of the majestic trees, stretching out as if to greet the approaching army. The swishing of boots cutting through long grass slowly faded away as the warriors stomped through the forest. They wove around the tree trunks like a flowing armored river.

"Does anyone know how much farther we have to go?" Hunter asked.

"Are we getting impatient?" Gameknight said with a smile.

But before she could reply, they were there. The village's crafter had stopped near the base of a small mountain. A dark opening sat at the base of the mound, its interior nothing but shadow. The whole army, maybe seven hundred strong, gathered around the entrance and stood quietly. Gameknight could tell that thoughts of what *might* happen were filling all their heads. Pulling a block of stone from his inventory, he jumped into the air and placed it under him. He then did it again so that he stood above all the warriors.

"I know all of you are afraid. I am as well," the User-that-is-not-a-user said in a loud, confident voice. "But I know if Xa-Tul is successful in bringing too many zombies here, he will crash all the server planes, and everyone—villagers, monsters, animals—everything will die. We must stop him, no matter the cost. I'm sure we will be outnumbered, but remember: zombies are dumb and cannot work together. We will also have the element of surprise on our side. Just stick to the plan and—"

"LET'S PLAY SOME ZOMBIE-RUN!" Hunter shouted in glee.

The rest of the villagers laughed, then cheered. A howl floated up from the forest. It was a distant wolf, and it reminded Gameknight of Herder's animals. They had disappeared after the young NPC had been captured and no one had seen them since. But now he could hear them in the distance, their proud voices coming from all around. Gameknight paused for a moment to listen to the animals, but he could tell they were not getting any closer. The wolves were keeping their distance. Apparently, without Herder, the animals preferred to stay only with their own kind. The User-that-is-not-a-user sighed as that last image of Herder, right before he was captured, filled his mind.

"I'm coming Herder . . . I'm coming," Gameknight muttered to himself; then he drew his two swords and held them high over his head.

"Let's do this!" he shouted, then jumped off the blocks and followed the crafter into the tunnel.

The army followed him through the twisting passageways. After the first turn, Gameknight noticed torches placed on the right side of the passage. Likely, they'd been put there by the villagers who had explored this tunnel long ago. The light buoyed the spirits of the soldiers, but they were still nervous . . . Gameknight could feel it.

Suddenly, a spider dropped down from the ceiling, falling right on top of a group of warriors. Gameknight drew his diamond sword, but two flaming arrows streaked through the air before he could even get close to the monster. The pointed shafts struck the beast in the side, causing it to burst into flame. A villager nearby struck the spider with his axe, extinguishing the flames as well as the creature's HP.

"We need to be careful," Gameknight said as he patted the axeman on the back. "Watch the ceilings for spiders and check the side passages for creepers. We don't want any explosive surprises."

They continued through the tunnel with eyes scanning for the shadowy movements of monsters lying in wait. Two creepers were found hiding inside alcoves, waiting for the best moment to jump out and ignite. The mottled green-and-black creatures were surprised when they saw the massive army flowing through their cave, and shocked when a dozen warriors turned on them as soon as they started to hiss. The creatures didn't stand a chance.

After five more minutes on the meandering path, they found themselves on the banks of a massive underground lake. Following its edge, they moved toward the orange glow at one end. As they neared, Gameknight could smell the smoke in the air, the ash biting the back of his throat with every breath. A river of lava flowed through a narrow passage and spilled into the edge of the water, creating a large, flat sheet of obsidian. The purple and black cubes seemed to glow in the orange light of the molten stone.

Gameknight cautiously moved across the obsidian. He could feel the warmth through his diamond boots; there was likely lava directly beneath the shadowy cubes on which he walked.

"Over here," the villager's crafter called, pointing to a flat wall of stone. He leaned his head against it as if listening to something.

Gameknight moved to the NPC's side and pressed his ear against the stone. He could hear the faint sound of zombies, their sorrowful moans just barely piercing the rocky wall.

"It's here," the User-that-is-not-a-user said. "Everyone get ready."

Stepping away from the wall, he scanned the area, looking for that one clue, and then he saw it: a single stone sticking oddly out from the flat partition. Moving to the lone block, Gameknight reached up and placed his hand on it. He then turned and glanced back at the huge collection of warriors that now filled the fiery, watery chamber.

"We will not yield, we will not surrender and we will not give up," Gameknight growled as he steeled himself for battle. "Remember the plan and stick to it, no matter what." He eyed Hunter and flashed her a smile, then glared at the stone wall. "Here we go."

And then he pushed the block, causing the stone doors to slowly grind open.

CHAPTER 30

THE IMPOSSIBLE BATTLE BEGINS

ameknight charged into the tunnel as soon as the stone wall had slid open far enough to allow him to pass. He didn't have to look behind to see if the others were following him or not. By the sounds of the thundering boots on the ground, Gameknight knew he was not alone.

Suddenly, a zombie stepped into the tunnel. Before it could make a sound, Gameknight attacked with his dual swords. An expression of shock covered the decaying creature's face as it realized who was attacking. But before the monster could utter a sound, the User-that-is-not-a-user took the last of its XP. It disappeared with a *pop*, leaving behind three glowing balls of XP and a piece of zombie flesh.

They moved down to the end of the passage, and when they stared out upon the zombie-town, Gameknight was shocked at what he saw. The cave was bigger than anything he'd ever seen. A collection of houses dotted the edge of the cavern, each a different size and made of different materials. It seemed there were only a few dozen of the structures lining the edges of the huge cavern. Most of the cave was open space, with a cratered floor and HP fountains sparkling at the center. But there was a strange appearance to these homes. The blocky buildings seemed old and unkempt, as if they hadn't been lived in for a long time.

At the center of the chamber was a wide, flat area with eight HP fountains distributed in a circle. The glowing green embers shot up into the air like holiday fireworks, then sprayed down upon the monsters that stood eagerly under the flow. At the center of the circle stood a massive zombie. He wore chain mail that glittered in the light of the HP fountains, giving the impression that his armor was covered with the rarest of emeralds, and a golden crown of claws sat on his square head. There was no mistaking him for any other zombie: it was Xa-Tul.

The zombie king was facing away from the invaders, staring down into the passage that led to the portal room. Out of the wide tunnel flowed what seemed like an endless parade of zombies, their numbers adding to the massive collection of monsters already gathered.

As their numbers grew, Gameknight could feel Minecraft itself slightly shudder, like it was having difficulties accounting for so many creatures on a single server. To the side, he could see a group of NPCs digging away at one wall, slowly expanding the chamber to make room for the increasing number of monsters. Within the group of prisoners, Gameknight saw one NPC who was skinnier than the rest, a tangle of black hair hanging around his head and shoulders. It was Herder!

The lanky NPC paused from his work momentarily, turned, and glanced up at the entrance. When Herder's eyes met Gameknight's, he smiled. The skinny boy pulled out a stone sword he'd kept hidden in his inventory.

"It's time to stop digging," Herder shouted, "and start FIGHTING!"

The other prisoners were shocked when Herder threw himself at the nearest zombie guard. Gameknight watched with pride as his friend slashed at the monster, dancing close to attack and then darting away to defend. The other prisoners cheered, then turned their pickaxes on their jailers, drawing the attention away from Gameknight and his villager army.

"Come on, everyone, Herder is buying us a little time," Gameknight said. "Everyone move quickly and quietly!"

The User-that-is-not-a-user sprinted down the steps that led to the chamber floor, then ran along the edge of the cavern toward Herder and the other prisoners. Suddenly, a sorrowful moan filled the air, followed by an angry growl.

"NPCs are invading!" a zombie voice cried. "It's Gamekn—"

The voice was lethally silenced by Hunter and Stitcher, but the partial alarm had done its job. Zombies from everywhere in the cavern moved toward the monstrous voice. Gameknight could see monsters shuffling between the few ramshackle houses that sat on the floor of the cave, their claws glistening in the green light of the HP fountains.

One stepped out in front of him. The User-that-is-not-a-user slashed at it with his two swords, then ran past. He knew those behind him would finish it off. Right now, he didn't care about fighting zombies. All he cared about was reaching his friend's side.

He curved around a house made of dirt, then another made of sandstone, until he emerged from the archaic structures and out into the open. Zombies growled when they saw him, but he didn't care. In the distance, he could see Herder swinging his stone sword with all his might, pushing the zombies back from the other NPCs. The prisoners had formed a large arc, with their backs to the stone wall, but the zombies were trying to get around their flanks and surround them. If that happened, the monsters would have an unbeatable advantage.

With every ounce of speed, Gameknight sprinted through the zombie rabble, pushing and kicking aside monsters with his swords and feet. With one great lunge, he shoved past the last of the monsters and reached Herder's side.

"Oh, hi, Gameknight," Herder said casually, as if it were nothing to be by his friend's side again.

"Herder, look out!" Gameknight screamed.

He grabbed the young boy and pulled him backward just as a golden sword swiped through the air, right where his head had been. The zombie growled as it glared at the User-that-is-not-a-user. Herder said something, but Gameknight didn't hear. He'd already shifted into battle-mode, his mind and body acting only on instinct. But instead of charging out into the mass of zombie bodies, he drew his enchanted bow, then placed blocks of stone under him until he stood far above the claws of the zombies. Firing as fast as he could, Gameknight999 launched flaming arrows into the crowd of monsters, attacking those nearest the prisoners. He didn't even feel as if he were aiming. His body just worked automatically, picking out the monsters that were the gravest threats and firing three quick shots to eliminate each one.

One of the monsters tried to claw his way up the pile of stone on which Gameknight stood, but Herder was there to finish off the monster. His stone sword flashed across the zombie in a blur of precision and strength. The User-that-is-not-a-user smiled as he watched the young boy take on monsters twice his size without the slightest hesitation.

Suddenly, more arrows fell down upon the monsters as additional archer towers were constructed and filled with expert shots; the rest of the army had arrived. Swordsmen and swordswomen charged forward, pushing back the monsters as even more NPCs began building additional fortifications from which to fight. They built walls with high towers and holes in the walls from where the archers could fire.

"Push forward!" Gameknight yelled, feeling the momentum swinging in their favor.

The warriors advanced, pushing back the zombies as they attacked on the ground, while behind them, the archers fired over the tops of their heads at the monsters. Swords clashed against claws as the zombies tried to fight back, but the villagers knew they had one thing going for them . . . they knew defeat was not an option. They fought with a ferocity never seen before in Minecraft, and it scared the zombies. Those at the front had nowhere to go and quickly fell under the villagers' insane onslaught. The zombies farther back saw how hopeless their situation was, and rather than advancing to meet the same fate as their fellow monsters, they fell back.

"Finish the defenses!" Gameknight shouted as he leapt down from his perch and pulled out his dual swords. When the other villagers saw his two swords, they cheered and pushed even harder, as if Smithy of the Two-Swords himself was fighting with them.

Villagers at the rear finished the defenses, adding more stones to the wall and building additional archer towers. Narrow openings were left in the walls that would allow the defenders to get back in but would force the zombies into tight spaces if they followed, where they would be easy to pick off.

The NPCs fought hard, giving their comrades time to complete the defenses.

"Everyone, get behind the wall!" the User-that-is-not-a-user shouted when it was complete.

The villagers turned and moved through the many openings, then spun around and attacked the monsters that pursued them. With villagers on both sides of the opening, they were able to fight two-against-one.

"Ready for Zombie-Run!" Gameknight shouted as he stepped back and put away his sword. Hunter came down from her archer tower and stood behind him. Crafter moved next to them, with Stitcher at his side.

"You ready?" the User-that-is-not-a-user asked.

They nodded their heads.

"Then let's do it!" Gameknight said.

He moved up to an opening, then yelled at the top of his voice, "ZOMBIE-RUN!"

Gameknight sprinted forward, with Hunter directly behind. Off to his left, he saw Crafter running between the zombies, Stitcher following him. When they were about five blocks from their defenses, Gameknight began placing blocks of TNT on the ground. Hunter lit them with flint and steel right after they touched the ground. Sprinting in a zigzag path, they placed a curving line of explosives amidst the monsters, each one blinking as soon as it was lit. They ran through the crowd of monsters, carving a circuitous path so as to reach as many of the approaching zombies as possible, then curved their way back to the wall. But when they reached their defenses, Gameknight was surprised to find that none of the blocks had exploded yet.

"Seal the walls," the User-that-is-not-a-user shouted.

Climbing up to the top of the wall, he stared out at the battlefield. The blocks of TNT were blinking, and went solid white, just as they were supposed to right before exploding. But instead of blowing up . . . it was like time stopped. The blocks just froze there, glowing bright white as if the detonation process was somehow paused. Minecraft was glitching.

"The server is starting to seriously lag," Gameknight said. "We don't have much time."

Suddenly, a huge wave of monsters flowed from the portal room and headed toward their position. It was easily another five hundred monsters. Now, an army nearly two thousand strong was charging toward the NPCs' defenses, all of them growling and wailing at the top of their voices. Many of the zombies had reached the defensive walls and were pounding on the stone barricade with their sharp claws. Gameknight knew there was no way they could stave off this attack forever; they were out-numbered three to one. He glanced down at the warriors behind the fortifications. They all had expressions of defeat painted on their square faces. Zombie-Run had failed. Every one of them knew what was rushing toward them; none of them stood a chance of survival.

"Seal the walls . . . fast," Digger boomed.

NPCs pulled out blocks of cobblestone, and quickly sealed any passage through the walls, leaving only holes for archers.

The User-that-is-not-a-user searched the crowd for his friend. When he saw Crafter, he sighed as despair covered his square face.

I failed, Gameknight thought as he watched the wave of fangs and claws about to crash down upon them.

CHAPTER 31
FRIENDS

Suddenly, a sound began to echo through the chamber. At first, Gameknight thought it was the zombies moaning, but as he stared down at the monsters that surrounded their position, he saw that they had all stopped pounding on the stone and were gazing up at the entrance to zombie-town. The chamber was completely silent, the zombies frozen in their places as the sound grew. Gameknight turned and glanced down at the villagers. He found all of them with confused expressions on their faces, with the exception of Herder. The lanky boy had a huge smile on his face, the look of defeat gone from his eyes, replaced with confidence.

"Herder, what is it?" Gameknight asked as the sound grew louder.

Herder stared up at the User-that-is-not-a-user and smiled, then answered with a single word that the other villagers did not understand. But Gameknight knew exactly what he meant.

"Friends."

Majestic howls filled the chamber. Gameknight turned and peered up at the entrance to the cave. A furry white tidal wave flowed out of the tunnel that pierced the perimeter of the zombie-town. Wolves by the hundreds charged down the steps and across the cavern floor. The proud animals ran so quickly that it was impossible to estimate how many there were, maybe five hundred, maybe a thousand. All Gameknight knew for sure was that it was the greatest sight he'd ever seen.

The wolves smashed into the zombie army, their strong jaws snapping at arms and legs as they tore into their adversaries. They wove between the monsters, attacking the decaying creatures as they sped by. Running straight toward the rocky defenses, the wolves fell on the monsters that had begun to pound on the fortified wall again, eliminating the attackers almost instantly. Once the zombies on the front ranks had been destroyed, the wolves turned and charged toward the rest of the army that was quickly approaching.

"Come on!" Herder shouted. "My friends need help. THIS ISN'T OVER!"

Herder pulled out his sword, opened the wall, and then charged out into the zombie army with his stone sword flashing like lightning. The entire army cheered, then rallied behind the lanky NPC with renewed courage. Gameknight ran to his friend's side and slashed at the monsters. Digger stepped forward with his two pickaxes. He swung them with such strength that any monster he hit just flew through the air, as if he had the *Knockback V* enchantment on his weapons.

Archers mounted the stone walls and fired down upon the massive zombie army. Arrows were notched to bowstrings and fired as quickly as possible. With the number of monsters in the cavern, it was almost impossible for them to miss their targets. But as the zombies were wounded, they quickly retreated to the HP fountains where they regained their HP.

"Focus on the closest monsters," Gameknight said. "Pass the word." The order was relayed as the warriors pushed forward.

Hunter appeared on Herder's left, her bow singing. Burning zombies danced about when struck by her arrows, but did not last long. She fired faster than Gameknight could swing his sword. Then Stitcher and Crafter joined them. The six friends stood shoulder to shoulder, refusing to yield any ground to the decaying monsters. The NPCs rallied, driving the monsters back even further. But as they fought, a menacing growl came from the center of the zombie-town. Gameknight glanced up and saw Xa-Tul glaring down at him, his massive golden broadsword in his clawed grip.

"Your time is almost over, fool," the zombie king growled. But instead of charging forward, the huge monster turned and ran for the portal chamber.

"Push them back!" Gameknight yelled. "The zombie king is running away!"

The NPCs cheered, and as villager and wolf fought shoulder to shoulder, they battled like their lives depended on it . . . which they did. Gameknight slashed at zombie after zombie, his dual swords tearing a huge path of destruction through the monster army. Between attacks, he glanced at the passage that led to the portal room.

All of a sudden, a loud, sorrowful moan rose up from the dark passage. It was then joined by more and more voices until hundreds of zombies all wailed together, their sorrowful moans bringing chills of fear to the NPCs.

Suddenly, the ground seemed to come alive with electricity. Tiny little sparks emerged from the cracks between blocks. At first, they were the smallest of things, like pale white fireflies on a warm summer evening flittering about on the ground. But then they became bigger . . . and angrier. The sparks grew into larger balls of electricity, zapping both monster and NPC alike.

"Ouch!" Gameknight said as a thin tendril of lightning climbed up from the ground and found a patch of exposed skin under his armor.

He reached down to rub his leg, then turned and looked at Crafter. The young NPC was scanning the surroundings, a look of shock and fear on his square face.

The thin snakes of electricity began to merge together into thicker bolts that shot up at the ceiling of the cavern. The brilliant shafts of energy struck the stone roof with the force of a giant's fist, causing blocks to explode and rain down from above. The lightning grew bigger and angrier as the bolts zigzagged into the air. It was as if they were trying to claw their way to the surface of the Overworld.

Many of the stone blocks began to shatter for no reason, bursting into clouds of sparks, the lines of code holding them together finally beginning to fail.

"Crafter . . . look!" Gameknight shouted over the din of battle.

"I know," Crafter replied as he dodged a zombie attack, then slashed at the monster, making it disappear. "Maybe this is the end?"

"No . . . it can't be," Gameknight said. "I refuse to be defeated. We can do this. . . . WE CAN DO THIS!"

The NPCs cheered and began to fight harder.

Suddenly, a purple mist formed in the air, forcing many of them to step back. The mist sputtered and flickered, then solidified. And suddenly they were surrounded by two hundred endermen, with Feyd, the king of the endermen, standing directly in front of Gameknight999.

CHAPTER 32
UNEXPECTED HELP

Gameknight held his swords before him and readied for battle. He flashed an angry glare at the tall skinny monster, then quickly looked away, knowing what would happen if he stared at the enderman too long.

"Feyd, king of the endermen," Gameknight growled. "I didn't expect you to be stupid enough to participate in this insanity . . . yet here you are."

"I haven't come to fight you, User-that-is-not-a-user," the king of the endermen snapped. "Xa-Tul is insane and will kill us all. The only way he can be stopped is if we work together."

A zombie stepped forward and lunged at Gameknight. He slashed at it with his iron sword, hitting it twice, then finished it off with his diamond blade. He was careful to not hit or bump into any of the tall, shadowy monsters. Most of the other zombies were cautious of pushing through the line of endermen to get to the villagers, but a few were foolish enough to try. Another zombie shuffled through barrier of dark creatures and dove at

Gameknight999. A pair of flaming arrows streaked through the air and hit the zombie before it could reach its target. The User-that-is-not-a-user finished it off quickly, then turned and faced Feyd.

"Why would you help us?" Gameknight asked as he scanned for more attackers.

"The zombie king thinks he is only destroying the villagers," Feyd explained. "But everyone will be killed if he is successful. We must stop him at all costs."

"What do you want from me?" the User-that-is-not-a-user asked, suspicious of joining forces with a sworn enemy.

Another zombie jumped at him. He kicked it hard with his diamond boots, then took the rest of its HP with three quick hits. The NPCs were now falling back as more and more monsters pushed their way through the line of endermen. The flow of monsters coming from the portal room had not slowed down, and in fact, it looked like it had actually increased. More bolts of lightning shot up into the air, striking the decaying creatures as well as NPCs. The press of the additional zombie bodies was forcing all of the monsters forward, toward the villagers.

Sparks of electricity crackled all around the chamber as random blocks disappeared from sight, thin ribbons of lightning shredding the blocks. But the strange thing was, the lightning was coming from the *inside* of the stone cubes.

"You must hit me so that my endermen can join the fight." Feyd said. "That is the only way we can help."

"You want me to add your endermen to the fight?" Gameknight asked. "Do you think we are fools?"

The dark creature shrugged as he glared at the User-that-is-not-a-user.

"You are losing," Feyd said. "You have no choice. In another minute, the server is going to crash. Look around you. The blocks are already starting to disintegrate."

Gameknight surveyed the chamber. He could see thick strands of lightning twisting up into the air, causing the blocks beneath them to just disappear. Huge rifts were forming across the chamber as gashes sliced through the stone, some devouring the zombies that stood above. Bolts of lightning shot out in all directions. It was chaos.

"Hurry!" the king of the endermen screeched. "Soon it will be too late. We must act now!"

Gameknight sighed. He knew the enderman king was right. They had no other choice.

"You better not betray me, or destroying you will be the last thing I do," the User-that-is-not-a-user said.

"You can trust me," Feyd replied in a high-pitched voice, a wry smile on his dark red face.

Gameknight laughed, then hit the dark creature with his iron sword. Feyd's eyes instantly began to glow bright white as he screeched an ear-piercing scream that made the zombies stop for just a second.

"NOW!" the enderman king yelled.

Suddenly, the shadowy monsters stepped up to nearby NPCs and wrapped their long, clammy arms around the villagers. With their weapons pinned to their side, the villagers were helpless.

"I knew I couldn't trust you!" Gameknight said as he struggled to get free of Feyd's grasp, but the long arms were like bands of dark steel.

"Just be quiet and get ready," the monster said quietly in his ear, then raised his voice to a shout. "Endermen, teleport NOW!"

Suddenly, the monsters were enveloped in a sputtering purple mist. They disappeared one by one—some of the endermen were clearly having difficulty teleporting as they vanished—then reappeared, then vanished again. Gameknight's vision blurred for an instant, and then they all materialized in the portal room.

"What's this?" Xa-Tul bellowed. "Is Feyd bringing Xa-Tul a gift?"

"Not quite," Feyd replied, then released Gameknight999 as the other endermen did the same. Suddenly, there were forty villagers standing next to forty endermen. "Endermen . . . attack!"

The shadowy monsters fell on the zombies, their fists a blur as they pummeled the zombies in the chamber. But with the glitchy server, the dark monsters were not able to teleport away from the zombies' glistening claws. The decaying creatures tore into the shadowy endermen with a vengeance.

"The zombies have been betrayed for the last time," Xa-Tul said as he drew his golden broadsword and stormed toward Feyd. But before he could reach the enderman, Gameknight stepped in his way.

"Villagers, attack!" Gameknight shouted over the growling zombies.

The NPCs fell on the zombies, fighting side by side with the endermen. Their swords blocked the vicious claws as the dark fists of the endermen smashed into the zombies. For the first time in Minecraft history, villagers and endermen fought as allies.

"The fool wishes to fight . . . perfect," Xa-Tul growled.

The zombie king swung his massive broadsword at Gameknight999, aiming for his head. But Gameknight had already moved. He ducked down, letting the golden blade slice through the air, just overhead. With his diamond sword, he smashed into Xa-Tul's chain mail with all his strength, landing three quick hits. Before the monster could respond, the User-that-is-not-a-user rolled to the left, then attacked an exposed leg. The zombie king screamed out in pain, then brought his broadsword down upon Gameknight's diamond weapon. He tried to raise his iron sword in defense, but was too slow. Pain exploded through his shoulder as his right arm went numb, his diamond armor cracking under the strain.

Gameknight stood up and slashed at the monster again, dodging to the left, then dancing to the right; but with all the creatures in the room, the User-that-is-not-a-user did not have enough room to move. He knew he couldn't evade that golden sword when squeezed by the crush of bodies around him. With all his might, he swung both blades at the monster, but the zombie's mighty broadsword came down on Gameknight's wrists, knocking his swords from his hands.

"Ha ha ha . . . all too easy," the zombie growled.

The zombie king then raised his massive golden sword high into the air for the killing blow. But as the monster began his stroke, Feyd dove forward and smashed into the zombie. The king of the endermen wrapped his long dark arms around Xa-Tul, then pushed him backward until the two mighty kings fell to the ground. They struggled, trying to gain an advantage as they rolled back and forth. But then Feyd pushed off with his long legs and caused the two monsters to roll forward until the top half of their bodies went through the sickly yellow portal, while their bottom-halves remained in this server.

"Quick! Break the portal," Feyd screamed as the upper half of his body began to teleport to the other server.

"What will happen to you?" Gameknight shouted as he stood and pulled out his diamond pickaxe.

"Just do it!" the monster screeched.

Gameknight gripped his diamond pickaxe, then put every ounce of strength he had into the swing. He smashed the obsidian block that made up the corner of the portal. Swinging again and again, he dug into the dark cube.

Zombie claws found his back and tore into him, but suddenly, Cobbler was there, pushing them back with his iron sword. Out of the corner of his eye, he could see the young boy slashing at the decaying beasts like an experienced warrior.

Swinging harder, Gameknight dug at the obsidian while the two monsters kings struggled, half of their bodies already disappeared and transported to the different server plane. And then suddenly, the dark purple block shattered. The sickly yellow teleportation field flickered for an instant, then vanished, cleaving the two monsters in half. Their lower halves lay still for just an instant, then disappeared as well.

Xa-Tul, king of the zombies, and Feyd, king of the endermen, were dead.

"We did it!" Cobbler shouted as he finished off the zombie before him.

"Not yet," Gameknight said. "Look around you."

Cobbler backed up and then glanced around. All the blocks around them crackled with electrical sparks as they began losing their shape and disappearing.

Suddenly, the cavern was filled with thunder. The NPCs and endermen in the portal room pushed forward and fell on the remaining zombies in the portal room, then ran up the steps to see the source of the thunder. Gameknight scooped up his swords as he ran up the steps, chasing a lone zombie. Two arrows stuck into the creature's back, causing it to burst into magical flames. It turned to growl at him. But before it could make a sound, a third arrow finished it off.

When he reached the massive chamber, Gameknight was greeted to more explosions as a few of the TNT blocks from the Zombie-Run finally detonated, tearing through the massive collection of monsters. The villagers and wolves had retreated back to their cobblestone walls, luckily sealing themselves in and keeping themselves safe from the blasts. The endermen that stood nearby glanced nervously at each other when they learned of Feyd's demise. Uncertain as to their fate, they all teleported away, leaving behind a flickering purple mist.

The zombies now covered the floor of the chamber. They pressed forward, edging closer to the NPC defenses, but the first blocks of TNT near the fortified wall detonated, keeping the creatures back. More explosions erupted across the cave as the TNT caught up with the server's clock, finally starting the Zombie-Run that Gameknight and Crafter had started. Huge blossoms of fire bloomed across the chamber floor, rending HP from zombie bodies and littering the ground with XP. As the number of zombies in the chamber decreased, Gameknight realized that the server was now able to recover from the system overload, and it began to work faster. With more explosions, and more zombies destroyed, the glitchy lightning from the blocks seemed to decrease until it was just the faintest of crackles. Suddenly, in a cascade of blasts, the remaining blocks of TNT detonated, destroying huge clusters of zombies with an explosive fist and extinguishing all the sparks from the stone blocks.

When the last of the red-and-white striped cubes had detonated, the NPCs and wolves flowed out from behind the walls and charged forward. Only a mere hundred zombies had survived Zombie-Run, and now the monsters were the ones that were far outnumbered. With a loud cheer, the villagers smashed into the remaining monsters, falling on them with a vengeance. The decaying creatures backed up, away from the villagers. Knowing they were hopelessly outnumbered, many tried to flee, searching for hidden tunnels in the walls of the zombie-town. Their moans were sad and terrified as they shuffled across the uneven floor in a vain attempt to escape.

Gameknight ran to the center of the cave, then banged his sword on his cracked chest plate, getting the villagers' attention. A few of the NPCs had captured some of the zombies and held them on the ground, swords ready to end their lives, while others were chasing monsters that were trying to escape.

"Let them go," Gameknight yelled. "Minecraft needs balance. We cannot destroy all of the monsters."

The villagers nodded, but the wolves were not so easily convinced, their growls filling the air. But then Herder whistled, the sound loud and piercing. The wolves stopped in their tracks, then turned and ran toward the sound, allowing the decaying monsters to run out of the chamber and into the dark tunnels that led deeper into the flesh of Minecraft.

Herder moved next to Cobbler, who was now limping, and helped him walk to the User-that-is-not-a-user. Gameknight surveyed the chamber, looking at the survivors of what could have been the last battle for Minecraft, pride welling in his heart. He reached out and put an arm around Herder's shoulder, pulling him in close, then did the same with Cobbler. The young boy groaned in pain, but the User-that-is-not-a-user could nevertheless see a huge smile on his young square face. The villagers cheered and the wolves howled with pride.

"We did it!" someone shouted.

"Minecraft is safe," another hollered.

Gameknight nodded, then released the two boys and stepped forward. The crowd grew quiet.

"Today, we saved all the lives on all the servers within Minecraft," Gameknight said. "It is a great day that will be remembered for a long time."

Everyone cheered, then grew quiet again.

"But the sacrifice was also great," the User-that-is-not-a-user added. "Many of our friends and family members lost their lives today, and we must not forget them."

The villagers nodded as they noticed the piles of items from the inventories of the deceased. They were spread all across the cavern, the number of piles shocking. Gameknight surveyed the chamber, then brought his gaze back to the survivors. Slowly, he raised his hand, fingers spread wide.

"Our friends and family did not die in vain," the User-that-is-not-a-user said in a loud voice. "They freed the prisoners taken by Xa-Tul and saved Minecraft from destruction. Our fallen comrades will be forever remembered for their sacrifice."

"For Baker . . ." exclaimed an NPC.

"For Cutter . . ." said another.

"And Farmer . . ."

"And Weaver . . ."

The litany of names flowed from the villagers as their grief surfaced and replaced their battle rage. Tiny square tears flowed from eyes as they mourned for their loved ones. Gameknight reached up and wiped his cheeks dry, then squeezed his upraised hand into a fist until his knuckles felt like they might pop. Finally he lowered his hand, the rest of the army doing the same.

"We must always remember," Gameknight added.

The NPCs nodded their square heads.

"Thank you all for coming and rescuing us," Herder said. "It's true; family is always there for you . . . and we are *all* family."

"Well said," Crafter added.

"I'll tell you all one thing, this place smells like rotten zombies," Gameknight999 said. "Let's get out of here and go back to our homes."

The villagers all cheered, then headed for the stairs that led out of the zombie-town.

CHAPTER 33
GOING HOME

Gameknight felt as if he were holding his breath as they traveled through the minecart network back to their own village. During the trip through the dark tunnels, he half-expected zombies to jump out of the shadows at any moment, or Minecraft itself to fall apart and disintegrate; he couldn't really believe that it was all over. But when they made it back to their own village, the User-that-is-not-a-user finally breathed a sigh of relief and felt himself relax, just a little.

"Is it finally over?" Stitcher asked. "Are all of Herobrine's monster kings finally gone?"

"There is still the creeper king," Gameknight answered. "But I don't think he wants anything to do with us. Oxus just wants to live his life with his creepers in their underground kingdom."

"Maybe that *was* the Last Battle then," Cobbler said.

"That's a very positive way to look at it," Crafter said. "I'm proud of you. I know your leg hurts and many of the NPCs from your village did not survive their captivity. You had a lot of negative there that you could have focused on, but instead, you chose to seek out the positive. That is fantastic."

Cobbler beamed.

"I learned something from watching all of you," the young boy said.

"And what was that?" Digger asked as he put his minecart in a chest next to the tracks.

"Well, I watched the way the six of you work together, and how hard you all worked to save Herder and save Minecraft," Cobbler said. "And I realized that you have people around you who care, and would do anything for you. You know, like how all of you fought to save Herder. When you have friends and family around you like that, then there is *always* something positive nearby. You just have to open your eyes and not be afraid to look."

"Well said, Cobbler," Crafter said.

"Yep," Stitcher added.

"Maybe I learned something as well," Gameknight said. "I didn't honestly think we were going to survive that battle. There were a lot of zombies in that cave, and I didn't really expect Zombie-Run to actually work."

"That might have been good to know when you had me running behind you amongst all those monsters," Hunter complained, then punched him in the arm.

"Ouch," he said. "Would you have followed me if I told you the truth?"

"Of course, you idiot!" she snapped and punched him in the arm again.

"Well, as I was saying before I was so brutally attacked," Gameknight said, then flashed a smile at Hunter, "I think I had a hard time seeing the solution to this problem because I was imagining everything that might be happening to Herder. I blocked a lot of you out because I was so afraid that I would fail, and I should have told you how I felt instead of just keeping it to myself." He paused to clear his throat, and to try to keep a tear out of his eye. "I should have confided in all of you, and instead I just kept my problems to myself. That was wrong, and I'm sorry."

"Well, since you did save all of our lives, and kept Minecraft from being destroyed, I guess we can forgive you," Hunter said, then punched him in the arm again, this time, much softer.

They all became quiet as the six companions stood there and stared at each other, taking in the moment, engraving it into their memories forever.

Suddenly, letters appeared in his head. *Son, what are you doing?* the words said as they scrolled through his mind; someone in the physical world was typing into the chat window in Minecraft.

Ahh . . . I was just checking in on everyone here in the village, Gameknight replied as he imagined himself typing the words on his keyboard. *Sorry, Dad, I should have told you I was going back into Minecraft.*

"What are you . . ." Hunter started to ask, but Gameknight raised a hand, silencing her. He was surprised it actually worked.

Anything going on in Minecraft? his father asked as he typed into the chat.

No, just the same old boring stuff, Gameknight replied. *Crops need harvesting, animals need tending, walls need repairing . . . nothing unusual.*

Good. I don't want you taking any more chances in there, his father said.

Of course not, Gameknight lied. *You know me.*

That's the problem: I DO know you. Now say goodbye. It's time to go.

OK, Gameknight replied.

He turned and gazed at his friends.

"I have to go," he said in a sad voice.

"When will you come back?" Hunter asked.

"I don't know. Maybe tonight," Gameknight replied. "We have a thunder storm coming our way in the evening, so I don't know if I'll be able to use the computer or not. But if I can, I'll be back online later."

"You know where we will be," Crafter said. "Hurry back. You will be missed."

Gameknight gave his young friend a smile, then turned and glanced at Cobbler.

"I'm sad that I have to go, but I'm more excited at the thought of coming back," the User-that-is-not-a-user said. "That's what I'm focusing on: not the leaving, but the returning."

"I get it," Cobbler said, "I really do."

"Good," Gameknight replied.

Just then, a sphere of light started to form around him. It grew brighter and brighter until all he could see was white. He felt hot and cold at the same time as tiny jolts of electricity seemed to dance all over his body. And then Gameknight999 was gone from Minecraft.

MINECRAFT SEEDS

All of the different biomes and structures mentioned in the book can be seen on Gameknight999's server. Just go to the book warp room on the survival server and you'll see the buttons for each chapter. We are in the process of adding a new survival server, and it will take time to move all the book warps to the new server, but you can go to the old survival server and see the book warps there. You can use the command */warp bookwarps*. I'll be building the creeper hives somewhere on the server so that all of you can see what I was imagining while I was writing. Maybe I'll try to make one of the burned-out forests as well, if that's possible. . . . Come to the server and find out.

For those without access to the server, I've listed Minecraft seeds for version 1.87. I don't know if they will work with Minecraft PE or if they'll work for version 1.9; you'll just have to try them out and see.

Chapter 1 - Desert Village: 3049493360113604773

Chapter 5 – Crafter's Village: on server

Chapter 6 – Savannah Village:
2958776707072848190
X= 112 Y= 73 Z= 132

Chapter 16 – Waterfall: 1628270989

NOTE FROM THE AUTHOR

I can't believe this is my twelfth novel. . . . Who would have ever thought this crazy ride would have lasted this long? All of you out there who are reading my books and sending me such kind messages through my website, www.markcheverton.com, I appreciate all your emails and try to answer every one. Be sure you type your email address correctly on my website so that I can send you a reply.

Since I began to Skype with schools all over the country (check my website for Skype information on how I can speak with you and your classmates about creative writing and all things Gameknight999), the number of stories that kids are sending to me has increased significantly. The creativity that I'm seeing is fantastic. Kids of all ages have such wonderful imaginations, and I'm glad to see that many of you are putting aside any fear of writing you might have and are putting quill to parchment. Please keep sending in those stories. I love reading them and I post every one to my website.

For those who want to say hello to myself, Monkeypants_271, or my son, Gameknight999, come onto the Gameknight999 Network. It is a Minecraft server open to all with a PC license. Quadbamber (LBE Gaming on YouTube) has done some spectacular work on this server. With his experience of Minecraft servers and plugins, new features have been added to the server that make it a great place to meet, talk about my books, and play Minecraft in a lot of different ways. You can challenge me to a game of paintball, or survival games, or maybe try some of the custom games we have created just for this server. If you log on, you will notice a positive attitude amongst most of the players, which I believe has been caused by Crafter, Digger, Hunter, Stitcher, and Herder: a willingness to help each other. People build cities *together* rather than going far out into the wilderness alone to build their own home. People share resources and trade goods and in general play *together,* instead of *against* each other. I hope this trend will continue.

If you see me on the server, come say hello. You can find information about the server at www. gameknight999.com. We'll be adding some new game features like Elytra racing and new paintball arenas, so check the website for server news and updates. The book warps can be found on the survival server just by typing */warp bookwarps.*

Keep reading, and watch out for creepers.

Mark

AVAILABLE NOW FROM MARK CHEVERTON
AND SKY PONY PRESS

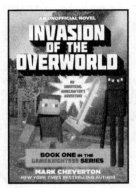  

THE GAMEKNIGHT999 SERIES
The world of Minecraft comes to life in this thrilling adventure!

Gameknight999 loved Minecraft, and above all else, he loved to grief—to intentionally ruin the gaming experience for other users.

But when one of his father's inventions teleports him into the game, Gameknight is forced to live out a real-life adventure inside a digital world. What will happen if he's killed? Will he respawn? Die in real life? Stuck in the game, Gameknight discovers Minecraft's best-kept secret, something not even the game's programmers realize: the creatures within the game are alive! He will have to stay one step ahead of the sharp claws of zombies and pointed fangs of spiders, but he'll also have to learn to make friends and work as a team if he has any chance of surviving the Minecraft war his arrival has started.

With deadly endermen, ghasts, and dragons, this action-packed trilogy introduces the heroic Gameknight999 and has proven to be a runaway publishing smash, showing that the Gameknight999 series is the perfect companion for Minecraft fans of all ages.

Invasion of the Overworld (Book One):
$9.99 paperback • 978-1-63220-711-1

Battle for the Nether (Book Two):
$9.99 paperback • 978-1-63220-712-8

Confronting the Dragon (Book Three):
$9.99 paperback • 978-1-63450-046-3

  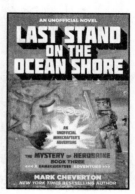

EXCERPT FROM THE GREAT ZOMBIE INVASION

A BRAND NEW GAMEKNIGHT999 ADVENTURE

Gameknight admired the amount of work the diggers had been able to do in such a short time. The crafting chamber looked as it had the first time he'd met Crafter, minus the minecart tracks; that was the next project to tackle. Weaver and some of the other young NPCs stood near him, all of them gobbling up his praise like candy.

"The circular room above looks fantastic," Gameknight said. "And these steps down to the floor of the crafting chamber are spectacular."

Weaver and the others beamed.

The kids had put in a wide set of steps at the opening to the cavern. They sloped downward, following the wall of the massive cave, then curved so that they spilled down to the center of the floor. Crafting benches dotted the chamber with chests placed along the walls. Each chest had a sign on it, signifying what was within: arrows for one, iron swords for another, leather armor and bows in another. Gameknight had convinced Smithy that they should begin crafting the tools of war, and everyone not on guard duty was either in the chamber, crafting, or in the mines looking for iron and coal and diamonds.

Closing his eyes for a moment, Gameknight listened to all the activity. It sounded just like Crafter's chamber, with the constant clatter of tools creating a blur of noise that was, for some reason, comforting. For the first time, Gameknight999 felt as if he were home.

"What do we do next?" Weaver asked. "The tunnels for the minecarts?"

"Exactly," the User-that-is-not-a-user replied. "We need a tunnel that heads straight to the closest village. Use all the iron left over from making swords for the minecart tracks. In no time, you'll have a minecart network that will connect all the villages together. After that we can—"

"Everyone, come to the surface . . . quick!" an NPC shouted from the top of the curving stairs.

Gameknight glanced up at the villager, but he'd already turned and left, the iron door slowly closing.

"Come on," Gameknight said to the kids.

He dashed up the steps, then burst through the iron doors. In seconds, he had shot through the round meeting chamber and was heading through the long tunnel. At the end of the dark passage, Gameknight could see a single torch illuminating a ladder that disappeared upward into a vertical shaft.

When he reached the ladder, he began to climb. He could hear the sounds of villagers below him, all of them climbing as fast as they could. As he moved, rung after rung, Gameknight thought about all the times he'd followed this path in the old Minecraft . . . or the future Minecraft, he wasn't sure. He missed those days. Gameknight had felt like a member of a community back then, but here, in this time, he felt like an outsider that was never fully trusted. Would they ever accept him?

He snapped out of his self-pity when he reached the top of the ladder. The vertical passage opened into the cobblestone watchtower, emerging from the far corner in the floor. Gameknight streaked across the floor and burst through the door. He sprinted across the courtyard and climbed the steps that led to the top of the fortified wall.

Surveying their surroundings, Gameknight found the sun rising over the eastern horizon. A rich orange glow stretched across the skyline as the sun rose higher and higher, the sparkling night sky slowly dissolving into a deep blue.

"Nice of you to finally make it," Fencer said, a tone of accusation in his voice.

"I was down in the crafting chamber, helping to—"

"Whatever," Fencer replied. "Just be quiet and look."

Out in the dark forest, a strange flickering glow seemed to move between the trees. It looked like the light of a fire, but no flames were visibly climbing up any of the trees. Instead, it seemed like the fire was walking through the forest as if it were out for an evening stroll.

"How can fire move through the forest like that?" Smithy asked aloud. "Is this another of Herobrine's tricks?"

Villagers blurted out many different theories, but none of them made much sense. As they argued, Gameknight sighed. He knew exactly what it was.

"I know what this is," the User-that-is-not-a-user said.

"Of course you do," Fencer said suspiciously.

"What is it?" Smithy asked. "Are they setting fire to our forest?"

"No, these are monsters approaching."

"Monsters? What kind of monsters can survive fire?" Fencer exclaimed.

"Blazes," Gameknight replied.

"What's a blaze?" Fencer cried. "I've never heard of those before. He's making this stuff up."

"I wish I were," he replied. "They're from the Nether, and they can throw balls of fire."

The forest was now brightening as the sun climbed higher into the sky. The timer on the digitizer in his basement was probably ready to go off. Once it did, his father's invention would bring him back to the physical world whether he was ready or not.

I hope I can at least finish this battle and help these NPCs, Gameknight thought. He knew he didn't have much time left.

"What's the Nether?" Smithy asked as he moved to Gameknight's side.

"A terrible place of smoke and fire and lava and nothing good," he replied. "We need to be ready. Everyone, keep moving around. If a blaze sees you standing still, they will shoot three fireballs at you. They always shoot a trio of balls, and they always flare bright just before firing. When you see them do that . . . move!"

"You seem to know a lot about them," Fencer said. "Why is that?" His accusatory tone hurt Gameknight.

"I've fought them many times. I know what I'm talking about. Now, everyone get to your battle stations."

No one moved. They just stood there, staring up at Gameknight999 with scowls on their faces.

"You heard him!" Smithy shouted. "Get to your stations and listen for instructions."

Archers climbed the ladders to the archer towers while other NPCs moved to the top of the walls. Everyone had a bow in their hands, with an arrow notched and ready. A silence spread across the village. Gameknight could feel the tension in the air; it was like a thread that had been stretched to its limit and was just waiting to snap.

Any minute I'll disappear.

And then the monsters came out of the forest and crossed the grassy plain that surrounded the village. They were all shocked when they saw at least thirty creepers scurrying towards them, with at least two dozen blazes floating behind. Each blaze burned bright with internal yellow and orange flames that seemed to make up the creature's bodies. Blaze rods spun furiously around within their fiery bodies, reminding Gameknight of some kind of evil helicopter.

"Remember, don't stand still. If you see a fireball coming toward you, duck behind a block of stone," Gameknight yelled. "The blazes will try to distract us while the creepers get up close and try to destroy the walls. We cannot let them do that."

The User-that-is-not-a-user turned and looked down into the courtyard. He saw Weaver and the other kids milling about, each of them wanting to get into the fight.

"Weaver, come here," Gameknight said. He had to be quick . . . any time now.

"You kids stay out of the way," one of the NPCs said. "This battle is for the adults. You little boys can't do anything helpful here."

"Weaver, don't listen to him and come here!" Gameknight shouted. "I have something that I need you to do."

The elder glared at Gameknight999, but he didn't care. They had to act fast, or a lot of NPCs were going to lose their lives in this battle.

Weaver dashed up the steps and stood at Gameknight's side. The other warriors cast angry glances toward the User-that-is-not-a-user, but he ignored them and just whispered into the young boy's ear.

"You think all of you can do this?" Gameknight asked.

Weaver looked down at his friends that were clustered around the village's well, then glanced back up to Gameknight999.

"No problem," the young boy replied, then took off running, his bright yellow smock a blur as he dashed down the steps.

He sprinted straight to the other kids and whispered something to them. The other adolescents listened intently, then nodded to Gameknight999. They took off running through the village, collecting what was needed.

"You know they can't help in this battle," Smithy said quietly to Gameknight. "They are too small and will only get in the way."

"I've learned not to judge people by their size, and rather, judge them by their courage," the User-that-is-not-a-user replied. "A smart villager once told me, 'Deeds do not make the hero; the fears they—'"

Before he could finish the statement, one of the villagers cried out.

"Here they come!"

The monsters stopped, just out of bow range, all except for the first wave of creepers. They crossed the grassy field quickly, their downturned mouths snarling as they approached the wall.

"Open fire!" Smithy yelled.

But before any of the archers could shoot, the blazes launched fireballs at the creepers. When the flaming balls of death struck them, they instantly started their detonation process, glowing brighter and brighter as they hissed.

"Shoot them!" Gameknight shouted.

He released an arrow, then fired again and again, but his shots didn't stop the ignition process. The creepers moved forward and continued to glow brighter and brighter until . . .

BOOM! . . . BOOM! . . . BOOM!

The first wave of creepers exploded, one after the other. Fortunately, the blazes had lit them too soon and they hadn't reached the village walls yet. Gameknight knew they would not make that mistake a second time.

"The next time, the creepers will destroy the walls," Gameknight said to Smithy. "The arrows should have stopped them from igniting, but didn't, for some reason."

"What? The all-knowing First-User doesn't know what happened?" Fencer mocked.

"Fencer, not now!" Smithy snapped, then turned back to Gameknight999. "What do you think they will do next?"

"They'll probably send all the rest of the creepers in the next wave, but they'll wait before igniting them," Gameknight said. "This time, the creepers will make it to the walls. And once those are destroyed, you can be sure more monsters will come storming out of the forest and walk right into the village."

"We have to do something!" Fencer yelled.

Just then, the young NPCs, lead by Weaver, came running back into the courtyard. They were each carrying multiple buckets and dipped them into the well, filling each with cool water.

Gameknight smiled.

"What?" Smithy asked. "You have an idea?"

"Yep," he replied. "When it's time, have everyone focus their arrows on the blazes. We'll take care of the creepers."

"We . . . who's 'we'?" Smithy asked.

But Gameknight didn't reply. Running down to the steps, he moved to the cluster of youths and spoke quietly to them. Each of them nodded their heads, though the User-that-is-not-a-user could see fear in their eyes. This was dangerous, but the element of surprise would give them the advantage.

"OK, let's do it," Gameknight said as he accepted a bucket of water from one of the boys.

He put the pail into his inventory and moved to the doors, the rest of the kids fast on his heels.

"All of you ready?" Gameknight asked.

They nodded their blocky heads.

"OK . . . let's go."

Quickly, he opened the door that barred the monsters' entrance to the village and let all the kids slip outside the walls. Gameknight then stepped out and closed the door behind him.

"What are you doing?" Fencer shouted.

"Get back in here!" Cobbler cried. "You're just a bunch of kids."

"Spread out and hold the line!" Gameknight shouted to the young NPCs. "Nobody runs and everyone waits until I give the word . . . understood?"

The kids turned and looked at the User-that-is-not-a-user and nodded.

"OK, here they come."

All the remaining creepers moved forward, but this time, the blazes held their fire until they had moved past the crater formed by the last set of explosive monsters. The blazes then opened fire, launching their flaming balls onto the creepers igniting them all. Gameknight could hear them hissing as they began to glow bright and come near. The creatures snarled, shuffling their feet faster and charging toward the line of young defenders. But none of the NPCs drew a sword. They just held their ground and waited.

COMING SOON:
THE GREAT ZOMBIE INVASION: THE BIRTH OF HEROBRINE BOOK ONE